"I remember in church, the preacher talked about Hell being fire and brimstone (whatever brimstone is). I always had the idea that Hell was hot and that if you were bad and went to Hell, you burned for eternity. I could imagine what that might be like as I have been badly sunburned and have burned my hand on the stove. After that night, my idea of Hell was being caught in a night-time stampede of crazed longhorns for an eternity, with the constant threat of being thrown, trampled, and gored. I still have nightmares about that night."

The Chisholm Trail to Dodge City

A Cornelius Howard Adventure

1880

By Kevin D. Howard

The Chisholm Trail to Dodge City

Front cover: The Chisholm Trail and wagon ruts southeast of Waurika, Oklahoma.
Back cover: Red River crossing at the old site of Red River Station.

ISBN: 978-1-7335766-0-4

U.S. Copyright Reg. No. TXu 2-129-906

FOR DISTRIBUTION INFORMATION CONTACT:
Prairie Sunrise, LLC
1405 4th Ave NW, #295
Ardmore, OK 73401

Colo14ers@aol.com

Preface

The Chisholm Trail first came into use as a cattle trail in 1867 when the railroad arrived in Abilene, Kansas. Early drovers crossed the Red River west of Gainesville, Texas at Sivells Bend or a little further west at Rock Bluff Crossing, near the mouth of Mud Creek. The trail went north around the west side of the Arbuckle Mountains and to Fort Arbuckle, on Wild Horse Creek. The Fort was on the north side of the Arbuckle Mountains. From 1867 to 1870, Fort Arbuckle was on the edge of the western frontier in Indian Territory. From Fort Arbuckle, the trail crossed the Canadian River near the site of Chouteau's Trading Post, south of present day Lexington, Oklahoma. Crossing the North Fork of the Canadian River in present day Oklahoma City, the trail angled northwest to cross the Red Fork of the Arkansas (now known as the Cimarron River) at Red Fork Station near present day Dover, Oklahoma. From there, the Trail went north to Kansas. The Trail from Texas to Kansas had been used by traders and freight wagons for many years.

At this time, Jesse Chisholm had a ranch two miles east of present day Asher, Oklahoma (south of Shawnee) on the north side of the Canadian River. He had trading posts at Fort Arbuckle, the old site of Chouteau's Trading Post, Council Grove (on the North Canadian River in Oklahoma City, at Council Road), and on the Arkansas River at present day Wichita, Kansas. Chisholm's Wagon Road went between these posts crossing the Cimarron near Red Fork Station before turning north to Kansas. The first herds of Texas cattle going to Abilene traveled past Fort Arbuckle for protection from the plains Indians and along Chisholm's Wagon Road from 1867 through 1870.

5

By 1871, Fort Sill had been established as the westernmost post in Indian Territory, and Fort Arbuckle abandoned. Beginning in 1871, cattle began crossing the Red River at Red River Station near Spanish Fort, Texas. This trail, to its junction with Chisholm's Wagon Road on the Cimarron, was originally known as The Abilene Trail. This new route, from Red River Station to Abilene, was soon referred to as The Chisholm Trail. The cattle trails had moved further west to the Red River Station crossing and now had a straight route north to Kansas across easy traveling, rolling prairie and west of the dense Cross Timbers. There was good grazing all along the way.

A stage line began in 1875 that ran from Caldwell, Kansas to Henrietta, Texas with stage stations along the way on the Chisholm Trail. There was also a stage line running from Arkansas City to Fort Sill.

By 1871, the railroad had extended south to Newton, Kansas, then on into Wichita in 1872. A branch of the Trail also went a little further west to Ellsworth, Kansas beginning in 1872. Herds of longhorns were driven up the Chisholm Trail to all four locations. In 1876, Kansas banned Texas cattle for the eastern half of the state leaving these markets unreachable. With no place left to go, Dodge City became the railhead for Texas cattle. The cattle drives now branched off the Chisholm Trail to follow the Cimarron River northwestward all eventually arriving in Dodge City.

The railroad reached Dodge City in 1872, and cattle began arriving in 1875 via the Great Western Trail which crossed the Red River at Doan's Crossing (near present day Altus). The Trail went north through the western side of Indian Territory. Between 1876 and 1881, cattle from both of these famous trails were arriving in Dodge City. A railroad was constructed in eastern Indian Territory and reached

Denton, Texas in 1873. However, it was cheaper to drive cattle to Kansas, so the cattle drives continued. In June, 1880, the railroad reached Caldwell, Kansas (in very southern Kansas) and drovers were allowed to ship their cattle from there. The Chisholm Trail north of the Cimarron River was back in business until 1887. By 1887 the railroads finally reached central Texas. The Unassigned Lands in Indian Territory opened to settlement in the Land Run of 1889. The Cheyenne-Arapaho lands were opened to settlement in the 1892 Land Run and the Cherokee Outlet lands (also mistakenly called the Cherokee Strip by most people then and now) were opened to settlement in the Land Run of 1893. The Cherokee Strip was a two-mile wide strip of land along the Kansas border which belonged neither to Kansas nor the Cherokees due to a surveyor's error. The day of the cattle drive was essentially over although there were a few drives into the 1890's.

The Abilene/Chisholm Trail roughly followed the 98th Meridian which was the dividing line between the eastern civilized Indian tribes and the fierce plains Indian tribes. At times there could be many herds all going north at the same time, with each herd strung out for a mile or more. With grass needed to feed the cattle as they went, the actual Chisholm Trail could be several miles wide at some points with the herds traveling side by side. As the traffic grew on the Trail, trading posts and stage stops appeared along the way.

This is a story about my great-grandfather.

7

Cornelius Howard

I am the 8th of 10 children. I was born in Johnston County, Tennessee in 1865 to James Carter Howard and Susan Shoun Howard. The folks didn't take sides during the War, so both Union and Reb soldiers raided and scavenged our place and Papa's foundry, so by the end of the War we had almost nothing. We moved to Indiana for four years where Papa rented a place and tried to farm. Things didn't work out there so Papa, Mama and nine of their ten kids moved to Texas in 1872 in two covered wagons.

The Comanche Indian Wars were fought mainly to the west and to the north of us until 1875 when the Comanche were moved onto a reservation in western Indian Territory. Some Comanches continued to raid in the Panhandle from the reservation until 1877. From the time we arrived and over the next several years, Papa would tell us stories he read about in the Burlington newspaper about Indian raids in the Panhandle not too far away. We never had any fights near us probably due to the thousands of cattle and hundreds of cowboys that seemed to always be going up the Chisholm Trail just west of town. They would start arriving in early March and continue through the Fall. The big herds tapered off around mid-summer.

There were many stories a little boy heard that were all about the ferocious and savage Indians that roamed the Territories just on the other side of the Red River. With only a shallow river separating us from them, there were many nights that one little boy didn't sleep too well and always had his trusty sling shot under his pillow.

We settled on the south side of the Red River near a little community called Liberty Chapel. Indian Territory was on the north side of the River. Momma said the area around

Liberty Chapel reminded her of the hills from where we came in Tennessee, but that was the only thing. Here, the summers were hot. Brutally hot. The ground where we lived wasn't so good either. It was tough for Papa to make a living, but it was all we could afford at the time.

It took us over two months to get to Texas from Indiana and probably the rest of the small amount of money Papa and Momma had. I don't remember much about the trip except I think I walked the whole way. Everything we owned was in those two wagons. I was in charge of watering the horses and the cow every time we stopped. I could only carry a bucket of water about half full, so in addition to walking the whole way, I made many trips down to many a creek.

Looking back, those wagon beds weren't very big at all. That means we really didn't have much amongst the eleven of us. Anyhow, the folks were starting over pretty much from scratch in 1872.

Not too long after we arrived, Papa told the older kids that they were on their own as he couldn't afford to feed them anymore. The ground was hilly, rocky and full of scrub oak with just a patch of grass here and there. Not very good for farming. There was no iron in the ground here like there was in Tennessee, so setting up another foundry was out of the question. I was almost 7 years old when we arrived in Texas. We worked from sunup to sundown to put food on the table. I was afraid he was going to kick me out too, but I was able to stay on another seven years.

I can't remember ever not working. Whether it was in the garden, doing chores or later working for my Uncle Dave at his livery stable. Papa always had jobs for us to do. I liked working for Uncle Dave because at least I got paid a little something.

We had one horse, one milk cow, a bunch of chickens, and usually two or three calves we'd get in the spring. It was my job from the day we left Indiana to make sure they always had water. We had a well that I seemed to have to pump morning, noon and night, just so those critters would have enough to drink. Well, and us too. We got our water out of the same well. It wasn't very good water. Sometimes it seemed to have a hint of salt in it but we got used to it.

We didn't have much land and the grass where we lived wasn't that good. There were several families in the area that were scraping out a living just as we were and didn't own much land either. We were all pretty much in the same shape. We all had the one milk cow and a few calves with no real place for them to graze. When I was ten, I went around to all of the neighbors and offered to take their milk cows each morning to a pasture area nearby and then bring them back that evening. I did this for a couple of years. No one had any cash money so I got paid in butter, vegetables and the like. When I started working for Uncle Dave, I had five or six boys about my age and younger working for me. We all took turns watching the milk cows and calves every day. As we got older, our chores and work at our own homes increased and none of us could babysit milk cows all day every day.

I would sometimes take our horse with the milk cows if Papa didn't need him, but he usually wandered off on his own. He didn't seem to like cows much. Sometimes it took quite a hunt to track him down in the evening. I got fairly good at tracking him. I practiced roping him and sometimes a cow or calf, and pretended I was a cowboy or gunfighter on the Chisholm Trail. On my way to that wild far off country called Kansas.

We kept our animals in our corral at nights. The calves always stayed near the milk cows during the day so they were never hard to find. Because of the calves, we kept them separate from the milk cow during the night so we could milk her for our own milk the next morning. Usually she wouldn't have too much milk in the evening with her being with the calves all day. Whenever we got new calves or had to get a new milk cow, it would take some training to get the milk cow to accept these orphaned calves. We would have to tie her up and put the calves on her until they all got used to each other.

I learned early not to get attached to any of the calves because the day would come when Papa would hang it upside down from a big tree limb, slit its throat to let the blood drain out and then, skin it, and cut it up. Every year at first frost you could kiss your calf good-bye. On the bright side, we'd have steak, roasts and jerked meat during the winter. Summertime fare was mostly vegetables from the garden, rabbits and squirrels.

Papa would get these calves cheap from the drovers passing through. Some of the herds would have cows in addition to the steers and heifers. Sometimes these cows would have their babies after the trail drive started. These herds would sometimes have a calf wagon that carried the calves during the day as they couldn't keep up with the herd. They were turned out with their mothers when the herd stopped for the night. Everybody around us always had two or three calves to raise during the summer thanks to the cattle herds coming through.

Spanish Fort, Texas

Just a few miles to the west and north of our house, big herds of cattle went by to cross the river at Red River Station. There was a big bend in the River just upstream that kept quicksand from forming here and the approaches to the Red on either side were also gentle and easy to cross. The crossing had been used for migrating buffalo for hundreds of years. The water in the channel was usually about 30 – 50 yards across although storms upstream could flood the River making the water much wider and sometimes impassable. Downstream not too far, the south banks rose high and steep. To the west the north banks rose high and steep. Salt Creek flowed north into the River from the Texas side. There was also a ferry at Spanish Fort.

The main crossing was east of Salt Creek. Once across the River, the terrain was generally flat with small rolling hills. The Chisholm Trail was on the west side of the Cross Timbers – an area of trees running southwest from Missouri all the way to Texas. The Cross Timbers were almost impenetrable. Also, the Trail was on the edge of the tall grass prairie so good grass was generally abundant through late summer for feeding thousands of cattle.

I later learned that the first cattle drives started well before the War and went up the eastern part of Indian Territory all the way to Sedalia, Missouri, the end of the railroad at that time. Missouri soon banned the cattle drives due to the ticks the longhorns carried. The ticks were fatal to their domestic cattle. So longhorns were no longer allowed in the State of Missouri. The Trail shifted to eastern Kansas and soon met with the same resistance. The abundance of trees and tall hills in the eastern part of Indian Territory made herding cattle through them very difficult plus there were Indian settlements and Indian ranches to drive them through or around. This trail was known as the Shawnee Trail and passed by Boggy Depot and Ft. Gibson on its way north. The Butterfield Stage once went this way from Ft. Smith to Boggy Depot and crossed the Red River on Colbert's Ferry. Passengers could ride the stage all the way to California. The railroad made it to Abilene, Kansas in 1867, so the cattle drives shifted fifty miles to the west crossing west of Gainesville and going up the Arbuckle Trail before joining Chisholm's Wagon Road at Fort Arbuckle. In 1871, the trail moved further west another fifty miles crossing at Red River Station on what was originally called the Abilene Trail, meeting Chisholm's Wagon Road at the Cimarron.

Cattle herds would have anywhere from 500 to 5,000 head. Most were around 2,500. It took ten or more cowboys to keep up with 2,500 head of wild longhorn steers. The herds had been going up the Chisholm Trail to the railhead in Abilene, Kansas – due north of us, and then also to Newton and Wichita as the railroads expanded southward. However, because of homesteaders moving west into central Kansas, Kansas had established a quarantine line north and south across central Kansas cutting off those rail lines in the eastern half of the state. Now the cattle drives were forced further west to Dodge City, Kansas.

The Chisholm Trail was the best trail for herding cattle north as water was no issue. All of the rivers in the Territory ran west to east and spring-fed creeks running into these rivers were plentiful. There were few nights, if any, of having a dry camp. The Great Western Trail another hundred miles or more to the west went through dry country all the way to Dodge City. In other words, the Chisholm Trail was perfect for driving cattle to market.

It was dry those years of the 70's. It seemed that Papa kept looking at me hard, especially during meal times, so I had a

13

notion that those cattle drives could be my way out and I'd better make the first move.

Just to the north of Liberty Chapel was Burlington, Texas. In 1876, the town had grown enough to apply for a post office. However, there was already a Burlington, Texas so they had to re-name the town. In the 1750's, the Taovayan Indians had a fortified settlement where the town is now. They were a branch of the Wichita Indian tribe. In 1759, Spanish soldiers attacked the settlement which was fortified and protected by some 6,000 Indians and a few Frenchmen. After a short battle, the Spanish retreated and left two of their cannons. By the mid 1850's, the settlement had been abandoned and settlers finding the two cannons, assumed there had been a Spanish fort there, so hence the new name – Spanish Fort.

Anyhow, back in those days with the herds going by from early Spring to late Summer, Spanish Fort was a wild town with four saloons. Killings and murders were not uncommon. It was the last civilization for dependable supplies and entertainment for the cattle drovers until they reached the railhead in Abilene, Kansas. Most of the cattle drives started in south Texas where the longhorns were wild and plentiful or where ranchers had joined together to raise a herd for the drive. All a person had to do, was hire some cowboys, gather 2,500 head or so, and head them north to Kansas. By the time they reached Spanish Fort, most of the herds had been on the trail for a month or more and were trail-wise and easier to handle. The roundups usually started in south Texas in February so the herds would have plenty of grass to eat on their way to Kansas in March, April and June. The cattle would usually put on weight during the drive as they were driven slowly and allowed to eat along the way. The first herds usually got the best prices after a long winter of no cattle shipments heading east. I also found out later that some herds leased

14

land and wintered in the northern part of the Territory known as the Cherokee Strip so they could be among the first arrivals to market in the Spring.

We always knew when the first herds arrived as the mooing, bellowing and bawling from the cattle was constant. Constant beginning in early March. Even at night. Those critters bawled all of the time. The herds with cows and calves were the worst. We got used to it to the point that when the herds thinned out in late summer, we had to get used to the quiet all over again.

Getting a Job

My sister Sarah had married a former Texas Ranger named Dave Utley. Dave now owned a livery stable where I had worked when I could for the past two years. One day, Papa told me to take the horse and, after school and after work, go to William Lovett's farm to get a milk cow he had bought from him. Our milk cow had gone missing. I was able to track it to the River. The Indians would occasionally cross the Red, steal some stock and then sneak back over to the Territory knowing we didn't have a lot of interest in following them. The Comanches had been raiding off the reservation as recently as three years ago, and some still snuck across at times to steal whatever they could herd or carry off. They didn't much like being confined to a reservation, especially now with the buffalo about gone. It was probably just a game to them.

The Chickasaws had territory directly across the river from us. They had been sent there back in the 1830's from Mississippi as one of the five civilized tribes. Some of the wealthier families had come on their own with their slaves and established good-sized farms and ranches. The poorer ones were forced to come later. We didn't think the Chickasaws were up to much thievery, but no one wanted to tangle with a wild Comanche who might be roaming over this way.

As I was riding through town that afternoon after leaving Utley's Livery Stable, the batwing doors of J.W. Schrock's Cowboy Saloon burst open and a cowhand came flying out. He hit the ground face first, rolled over and was up in a flash. As he wheeled around, he had a gun in his hand, but there was a man in a dark broadcloth suit standing in the doorway who shot him. Twice. I had stopped just short of the action and was fixin' to ride on to Lovett's when I heard a nearby cowboy say, "Boss ain't gonna like this. We were already a man short." I eased my horse over to the cowboy and asked who his boss was and where could I find him? He looked at me like I was some 14 year old kid (I was), grinned real big and said, "Mister, head northwest of town for three miles. When you find some of those longhorned steers, you'll find him. His name is Porter. We're headin' that a way. You're welcome to ride along with us."

Although down south of Spanish Fort where we lived was rough and hilly, the land northwest of Spanish Fort was flat and had plenty of grass. I guess it was part of the Red River flood plain. The river must have meandered back and forth over a huge area over the years. This area northwest of town had several thousand acres and there was plenty of room for several herds to stop over and graze before crossing the Red. I saw a vast herd of longhorn cattle of various sizes and colors. Some had horns six or seven feet wide. Most weren't quite that wide. Some cattle were grazing and some were laying down. On the west side of the herd were two wagons. I guessed one was the wagon that carried the food and supplies for the drive. The chuckwagon. It had a big canvas sheet spread over the end and held up by poles, kinda like a porch. We rode over that way. There was an older gentleman by the wagon who must have been the cook and several cowboys were sitting around.

"Sandy just got hisself shot. He won't be going' on to Kansas," the cowboy I met on the street said casually.

"That's not surprisin', Charley. Who's this young feller ya have wif ya?"

"Howdy," I said. "I'm looking for the trail boss name of Porter." I didn't know if Porter was his first name or his last name.

17

"And who might you be?" asked the cook.

"I'm lookin' for a job," I replied as I sat up straight and tried to look older and bigger than I was.

"Well, yonder he comes." I turned to look and in rode a solemn looking man on a tall coal black horse. He had a dark beard and blue eyes and wore wheat colored jeans, a light blue shirt, and a brown vest. His felt hat was pulled down low. I'd guess him to be in his mid-thirties.

Cookie said, "Boss, this here young feller is a lookin' fer a job. Charley here says that Sandy just got hisself shot. I guess he won't be ridin' wif us anymore." The trail boss looked me over very slowly from head to toe and didn't say a word for a long while. I tried to look him right in the eye. Then I started to get embarrassed. Maybe I was too young for this idea. I was about average height – about 5' 7" but didn't have much meat on me. I probably weighed close to 120 pounds.

Finally he said, "Can you ride, son?"

"A little." I had heard stories of what happened to people who said they could ride. The cowboys would sometimes rope and saddle the wildest buckin' horse they had to see if you really could ride.

He sighed. "Tell you what, son. Rope that yellow paint over there, and then go bring that black and white steer down there by the creek back into the herd." I heard someone chuckle. I was being set up. Well, I wasn't planning on being anybody's entertainment.

First problem was I wasn't that good of a roper. I had practiced on the milk cow herd and our horse, but none of them was ever that interested in getting away. We only had the one milk cow and I really never had to rope her – just rattle a bucket and she'd come trotting in to the barn. Of course, we boys had always played cowboy and practiced roping fence posts and the milk cows, but I had never roped a live animal that didn't want to be roped. Anyway, I had asked for it, so there was no backing down now. I picked up a rope laying on a saddle and walked over to the remuda where all the ponies were being held. Sliding under the rope that made up the corral, I eased up to that yellow paint pony talking easy like we were old buddies. Making a noose, I swung it just once and it settled easily over the pony's head. That was no big deal, I thought. So far, so good. I led the pony over to where the men were. One of them said, "You can use that saddle." I saddled the paint pony and he never moved a muscle. Maybe the trail boss had selected a gentle gelding for me to ride given the fact I was so light and so young. I swung up in the saddle and soon found out otherwise. That pony took off, stopped all of a sudden and then swapped ends faster than a bolt of lightning. I almost fell off, but I had ahold of the saddlehorn with my right hand, the reins in my left and a death grip around his ribcage with my legs. The stirrups were just a touch too long and were of no use. All of a sudden that paint pony started jumping like there were cockleburs under the saddle. I had heard that paint horses could be somewhat ornery.

I was still able to hold on. If I fell off, my cattle drive and my ticket out of Liberty Chapel was over. Then I got mad. I jerked the reins back so he couldn't have his head and started kicking that jakeleg pony with both heels. I didn't have any spurs on, but then that pony took off like he was the last one in a race and was determined to win it all. I leaned forward, still with the death grips with my hand and legs. I then started flailing him with the end of the reins.

First to the right side of his neck and then the left. I'll teach you to try to throw me, you stupid little . . . !

After about a quarter of a mile, he slowed down and I was able to turn him back toward the wayward steer. My plan was to get behind the steer and kind of ease him back toward the herd. He saw us coming and evidently had other ideas. He took off and headed south at a trot away from the herd and toward the creek. I gave the paint a little kick and it was soon apparent that this wasn't his first chase after a steer. He took off with a lurch that almost toppled me off over his back. So here we go – at full speed. I'm almost laying flat on my back with my heels up around his ears. I'm finally able to sit up and lean forward and, we go after that steer. The paint gets behind him and charges toward him.

Generally, most cows will turn and run when something or someone is after them, especially a man on a horse. Not this steer. He turns and comes right at us! The paint (and me) are taken by surprise. The paint lurches sideways and I fall off and hit the ground. Then the steer is after the pony. The pony turns tail and flees back toward the remuda. The steer realizes it can't catch the pony, but then he turns, sees me, and starts to come after me. Uh-oh! Well, instead of airin' out my lungs, I thought I'd better move fast.

I look around for a tree. There's a big live oak nearby, but no way can I get there and up and away from the steer's razor sharp horns in time. I see a big limb laying on the ground near my feet. It's about as long as I am tall and as big around as my arm. I pick it up. All of a sudden I get mad again. Except this time, real mad. Mad as a hornet! I've always had a bit of a temper. It probably had to do with my given name of Cornelius and the many fights that name caused me. Here I was trying to get away from home, get a man's job and now I was about to get killed by some stupid steer. C'mon, big fella, I'll be your huckleberry.

About that time the steer was almost upon me, his head went down to butt me all the way to Indian Territory. At the last second, I took a step to the side and swung that tree branch down low with both hands as hard as I could. It caught him right on the end of his nose. His nose hit the dirt and his horns plowed into the ground and stuck – and he flipped clean over. He did half a somersault and landed flat on his back. I ducked back just in time to keep from getting my brains kicked out as his flying hoofs sailed by over my head. I stood there still gripping the tree branch ready to swing it again. I was so mad I was shaking. My hands were numb from the shock of the blow and my arms were tingling all the way up to my shoulders. The steer rolled over, rose slowly to its feet and gave me a look that I will never forget. It was like 'how'd you do that?' He shook his head as if to clear it and trotted back to the herd.

I hadn't noticed that the trail boss had ridden up behind me. I saw him shove his pistol back into his holster. He gave me his hand and I stepped into the stirrup and swung up behind him. We rode back to the wagon. All of the cowboys and even the cook had big wide grins on their faces. I slid off the horse and the trail boss dismounted. "What's your name, son?"

I decided right then and there that I wasn't going to be taking any grief over the name Cornelius. "Cory", I replied. "Call me Cory."

He nodded at Papa's horse, "That's not much of a horse."

"It's Papa's."

"Take the paint. We leave at first light."

I decided to ride Papa's horse and save the paint for tomorrow, so I turned back to town and headed back to the livery stable to tell Dave I was heading north to Kansas tomorrow.
"You may never see that pony again, Boss," remarked Albert.

Porter replied, "Oh, yeah, he'll be back. He's got spunk. He'll never quit and he'll never give up. Tell Hollis that he can use Sandy's gear. I bet the kid shows up with just the clothes on his back."

A Texas Ranger

Dave had been a Texas Ranger and I loved to hear him tell stories of the chases and fights he'd been in. Tales of the outlaws and Indians he had killed or brought to justice. I never knew if the stories were real or made up. I assumed they were a little of both. Dave was a good story teller.

Dave was leaving the livery stable for the day when I rode up. "Dave, I just got a job on a cattle drive and I'm leavin' tomorrow for Kansas."

"Didja now? What's your pa going to say about that?"

I hadn't given that much thought. I just figured he would be glad to have one less mouth to feed. "I guess I'm fixin' to find out."

"What kind of weapon are you taking with you," Dave asked. Now that was one thing I hadn't thought about yet. "You'll be riding through Indian and outlaw country. There's not much law in the Territory. You better have a weapon in case you have to defend yourself."

"I have a .32 caliber Remington single shot rifle that I use for rabbits and squirrels," I replied realizing it wouldn't be of much use against outlaws or wild Indians.

"Come with me to the house," and Dave turned to walk down the street.

My sister Sarah, Dave's wife, was bringing water to the house from the well. I told her I was leaving with a cattle herd for Kansas in the morning. "What did Papa say?"

"He doesn't know yet."

She frowned. She was my closest sister, partly because I liked to spend so much time with Dave. I was at their house every chance I got. Once we were in the house, Dave came out of a back room carrying an old revolver. It was a single action .44 caliber 1858 Remington revolver cap and ball gun with a 5 ½ inch barrel. Originally you had to put in powder, a patch, and a .44 caliber round bullet, and tamp it down just like an old muzzle loader. Then you put percussion caps on each of the six nipples. When the hammer hit the caps the gun fired. Dave handed me the gun. "Cornelius, back in '72 when .45 cartridges first came out, I converted this old revolver so it would shoot the .45 cartridges. Take the cylinder out like this." He halfcocked the gun and pulled the loading lever down, so the cylinder would roll out into his hand. He removed the plate covering the cylinder and showed me how to load the cylinder with five cartridges. He then covered the cylinder with the plate, slid both back into the revolver, lined the cylinder up with the hammer and secured it all by pushing up the loading lever and locking the lever back in place.

"Although this is a .44 caliber revolver, with the conversion cylinder it now shoots a .45 Long Colt cartridge," Dave instructed. "I always ride with a .44 pistol since those cartridges will go in my Winchester .44-40 as well. These .45s won't. I couldn't afford another pistol, so I converted this old gun to a .45. I always took this as an extra pistol in my saddlebag just in case. You can tell the difference between the two cartridges. See how the .44-40 cartridge has a little shoulder to it – the base is bigger around than the bullet end here. The .45 is a 250 grain bullet and the .44 is only 200 grain. Be sure you don't get them mixed up. The .44s won't be accurate in a .45 pistol since they are a smaller diameter. The bullet won't spin down the rifling of the barrel properly. Also, a .45 cartridge won't fit a .44

pistol and will jam a .44-40 rifle since the cartridge is bigger around. "

"Here, you take it and leave the squirrel gun at home. Here's some cartridges and an extra cylinder. Keep both cylinders loaded and with a little practice, you will be able to swap out cylinders in no time. Let me get my old holster. It has a little holster attached to it to carry that extra cylinder. Keep it loaded." Dave went back into his room and soon came out with a very worn holster. We had to cut an extra hole in the belt as it was too big to go around me with me being so skinny. We shook hands. That was the first time I had ever shaken hands with anyone. "Cornelius, best to wipe your gun down every night, a cattle drive can be a might dusty, and clean it real good every time you shoot it. That black gunpowder can foul up the rifling in the barrel after so many shots and the bullet won't spin properly. If the bullet doesn't spin right, the gun won't be very accurate."

I had shot Dave's Colt .44 many times but had never shot this 1858 Remington. I shook the box of shells. It wasn't full. No time to practice now.

I said my good-byes. A tear rolled down Sarah's cheek, "Don't cry, Sarah." I mounted the horse, took up the reins of the paint and headed for Lovett's to get the new milk cow.

Annie Elizabeth Lovett

I rode, with the paint pony in tow, down the lane to Lovett's barnyard. Lovett had a little girl, Annie. She was a pest. She was always hanging around, making eyes at me. Giggling and carrying on. She was seven years old. I found out her middle name was Elizabeth so I always called her Lizzie just to tease her.

"Howdy Mr. Lovett. I've come for the milk cow."

"Nice lookin' pony you have there, Cornelius. Step down and come in for a bite of supper." I spied Lizzie peeping through the screen door.

"No thanks, Mr. Lovett. I just hired on to a cattle drive heading to Kansas. We're leavin' at first light, so I need to get back home and pack my few things." I thought I heard a little shriek. I looked at the screen door again, but Lizzie wasn't there.

I got off Papa's horse and we walked over to the corral where there were several milk cows. Mr. Lovett led one of the cows out of the corral and handed me the halter rope. "You be careful, son. It's rough country between here and Kansas."

"I will Mr. Lovett." I looked around and there was no sign of Lizzie. "Tell Annie good-bye for me."

"I sure will."

I got back onto the horse, and leading the paint and the milk cow, I turned around and rode back down the lane. As I neared the road, I heard Lizzie sobbing. She had run down to the end of the lane before me.

"Cornelius Howard," she cried. "You better take real good care of yourself and come back to me. I'm gonna marry you!"

I waved and rode on. Well, she was cute as a button!

Goodbye

It was almost dark when I got home. I put the milk cow and the horses in the lot. I unsaddled Papa's horse and rubbed him down a little. Then I got to working on the stirrups of the saddle on the paint – I assumed I was going to get to use that saddle as I didn't even have one. The previous rider had longer legs than me, but in no time, I had the stirrups adjusted just right. I hung the saddle on the side of the corral and rubbed down the paint as well. I forked some hay into the manger for all three animals and headed toward the house.

Eleven year old brother Johnnie came running out, "Whatcha doin,' Corny?"

I grabbed him and held him upside down. "I'm shakin' all the meanness outta you, child!" I swung him around and around until I knew he'd be pretty dizzy and then set him down. He staggered toward the house, falling down a few times. "Corny, you're a no count chiselhead!"

"Whatchu boys a-doin"? eight year old little sister Ida asked as she stood on the porch.

"We're looking for cooties," I replied. "Do you have any cooties on you?"

A look of fear crossed her face.

"Raise your arms up high, let me look."

When she did I grabbed her and tickled her good under her armpits, "there's lots of cooties under here!" Then I picked her up and tickled her ribs good.

She laughed so hard, she almost couldn't breathe. "Stop it C.H." (She always called me by my initials for some reason I never knew). I picked her up and gave her a big squeeze – I've always been partial to my sweet little sister. And then I gave her a big kiss on her cheek.

It was going to be a long time before I saw her again.

Entering the house, Mama was putting supper on the table. Papa was sitting in his chair reading the paper. He had just got in from working in the garden. It was planting time and we had to grow most of our own food. Having no plow or plow horse, we worked the ground by hand. He looked tired. "Did you get Lovett's milk cow, son?"

"Yes, Papa. She's in the lot."

"Where'd you get the gun?" He glanced at Mama.

"Dave gave it to me." I unbuckled my gunbelt and laid it on the bed in mine and Johnnie's room.

"Cornelius, please help me set the table," Mama asked. Mama's faded calico dress was very worn, but I never heard her complain. She always had something good to say about any situation. Papa said that even when the Rebs and Yanks took everything we had in Tennessee and burned what was left, she'd always say, "At least we're all alive and healthy."

I got the dishes and silverware out of the cupboard and placed five settings around the table. With the older kids gone our big table looked pretty barren with just the five of us now. This was going to be harder than I thought. Actually, I hadn't thought much about saying goodbye to everybody.

Mama put mashed up taters with milk on the table, along with some dried roast beef, and canned peaches. It being mid-March, we didn't have any fresh vegetables yet. The taters could keep quite a while in the root cellar. "Papa! Come to the table," Mama called.

Papa got up stiffly from his chair. He was only 51 years old and feeling everyday of it. "Cornelius, say grace for us tonight".

I thought now was as good a time as ever, "Lord, thank you for this food which Mama has prepared. Bless this house and everyone in it – and please be with me and keep me safe as I drive cattle to Kansas starting tomorrow. In your name we pray. Amen." I raised my head and opened my eyes to find four pairs of eyes staring at me.

"What did you say, Cornelius?" they all asked at once.

"I got a job today to help drive a herd of steers to Kansas. I was in town today on my way to Lovett's when there was a shootin' at the Cowboy Saloon. A big mean looking man in a black suit threw some cowboy out into the street and then shot him. Twice. I heard someone say the drovers were going to be short-handed on the drive now so I went out to the herd and asked for a job. It's time for me to start payin' my own way. We're leavin' at first light."

"But Cornelius, you're not old enough to go on a trail drive," Mama cried.

"And it's through Injun country. You'll probably get scalped!" Johnnie exclaimed all wide-eyed.

Papa never said a word.

No one ate much supper that night. We put the little ones to bed. "Will I ever see you again, C.H.?" sweet little Ida whimpered.

"Of course, you will." I tousled her hair and kissed her again on the cheek. "I love you, little sister."

I went to my room to gather my things. That didn't take long. I didn't have much and hardly anything that needed to go on a cattle drive. I had a pocket knife I had bought with the money I had earned, a coat, a shirt, one pair of pants that I usually wore on wash days, and two pairs of socks. Johnnie was watching me with big bleary eyes. "Johnnie, here buddy, you can have my slingshot. You and the boys take real good care of the neighbors' milk cows while I'm gone. You're in charge of them now."

A smile came to his face. He took my slingshot, held it tight against his chest and rolled over. "Bye bye big brother." He was soon fast asleep.

We had an old woolen army blanket that we'd use when we spent the night out by the creek. "Mama, is it OK to take this blanket with me?"
"Yes, dear. Is there anything else you need?"

"I don't think so." I couldn't think of anything we even owned that might be useful on a cattle drive. "I'll be leavin' before sun up. Good night." I rolled my things up in the blanket along with the box of cartridges Dave had given me and tied it up with a small cord.

"We'll be up to see you off."

I went to bed, but of course couldn't sleep. Today had been full of excitement and now a new adventure was fixin' to start. I couldn't shut my mind off.

Eventually I did fall to sleep only to wake with a start. I was always pretty good about waking up on time. Mama always said I had an inside alarm clock, but it wasn't time to get up. The sliver of the moon was low in the sky, and I know it didn't set until right before sunup, so sunup was still a couple hours away.

I was wide awake so there was no use going back to sleep. I got up, got dressed, buckled on the .58 Remington and put on my hat. There was a scabbard on the saddle, so I picked up my .32 Remington rifle and walked outside.

Leaving the bedroll on the porch, I went to the lot to saddle the paint. He was just a little bit feisty, but settled down enough for me to get him bridled and saddled. We went over to the porch. Mama and Papa were standing there. I tied my blanket roll to the back of the saddle. Mama had been crying. "My boy is all grown up. Please be careful."

"I will Mama."

Papa thrust out his hand, "Be careful son.

That was the first time I shook Papa's hand. On March 2, 1880, I left home. I was 14 ½ years old.

Crossing the Red
Tuesday, March 2, 1880

Since moving to Texas, I had never been out of Montague County. To be honest, I had never been more than 5 or 6 miles from home, much less across the River into Indian Territory. It was about 6 miles out to the herd from our house. Since it was still quite early, we just walked – me on the paint. For some reason, I think he sensed the solemnness of the occasion, for that was probably the only morning I ever got on him that he didn't crow-hop even a little bit.

We arrived at the camp as the drovers were getting up. I could smell bacon frying and coffee. "Come get you some flapjacks, son," Cookie said as I rode into camp. You can eat again even if you've already et. We need to fatten you up some." He handed me a plate with three flapjacks on it and a couple pieces of bacon.

"Wow, this looks great."

"Good grub makes for a happy outfit, son. I was able to make flapjacks with some eggs I picked up in town. They won't last long out on the trail. Here's ya a cup of hot coffee."

Now Papa never drank coffee although Mama and everybody else I knew did. Papa drank tea, hot and cold. Papa mainly liked cold spring water. Except for wintertime, the coldest he usually got was well water cold. I took a sip of that hot coffee and damn! It burned my mouth something awful! My tongue felt like sandpaper for a week. Oh, and it was oh so bitter! It tasted awful. I never took another sip of coffee for the rest of my life.

"Good morning, Cory." It was Porter, the trail boss. "You'll be riding left flank today. The flankers push the cattle and keep them moving from the sides. Swing riders ride near the front and about halfway back. They keep the cattle moving in the right direction. Albert usually rides point which is leading the steers down the trail. We have a man, Harley, who rides drag at the tail end of the herd and pushes all the laggards to keep up. Harley's getting' on in years and doesn't like galloping or trotting ponies so he just walks along behind dust and all."

"We'll be crossing the river soon. You get on the upstream side of the herd and don't let any get by you. If any come your way, let them drink and then just push them on into the water. This here is Albert. He's our ramrod. Number 2 boss. He'll be instructing you on what to do and how to do it as we go along. You'll meet the rest of the men over the next few days. What's that you have in your scabbard?"

I handed him the rifle, "It's a .32 caliber Remington."

"Octagon barrel, single shot falling block. Nice little gun. Well, you won't have much use for such a light gun out here. Put it in the chuckwagon and maybe Cookie can use it for rabbits and such. It's not too loud and won't scare the herd. We'll give you a Winchester .44-40, if you need a rifle. Now come with me to the remuda."

"You will have four ponies to use. The yellow paint, that sorrel over there with the two white forelocks, the black there with the star on its forehead, and that palomino over on the other side. You will need to swap out your ponies every time you come in. We generally stop at midday to let the herd rest and graze. You'll change ponies then. Then at the end of the day, you'll change ponies again if you ride nighthawk. Rotate your mounts so that they are always fresh when you need them. Any questions?"

"I had assumed I could use the saddle from yesterday? I don't have one."

"Yes, that was an extra one. We lost a hand two weeks ago and that was his saddle. Now with Sandy getting shot last night, we have another extra one. Consider this one yours until we get to Kansas."

"Thank you, sir!"

Porter went off to talk to the other hands having breakfast. It was still dark, but the fingers of the oncoming sunrise were just starting to appear.

"Cory, welcome. My name is Albert Romanstine. I'm the ramrod or segundo. Second in charge. My job is to see the work gets done —meaning the cattle get to Kansas fat and in good shape."

"If you're the one to see that the work gets done, what does Mr. Porter do?"

"Porter is the trail boss. The big toad in the pond. He's responsible for the entire herd. He's everybody's boss. The owners of the steers have hired him to take their cattle to market. He has hired us to help him. He'll ride ahead of the herd each day, determine which way we go and where we stop during the day and for the night. He'll check on any other herds in the vicinity so we don't all run into each other. He's always on the move and almost always out of sight. You will usually only see him in the mornings at breakfast and in the evenings at supper. We go from dawn to dark. And then we always have a couple of men riding nighthawk at night."

"What's a nighthawk?"

"Well, Cory, there are actually two types of nighthawks. One is the drover who is assigned night duty to circle the herd, make sure none wander off too far during the night, and see that no wild animal or rustler gets them. If the weather is bad, we'll use more nighthawks to try to keep the herd calmed down."

"The other kind of nighthawk is actually a type of hawk. You'll hear it just before sundown and during the night. It makes a certain chirping sound when it flutters its wings, then it will dive down to catch some insect flying in the air. When it does that, you hear a kind of 'whooshing' sound. You'll hear it soon enough."

I was soon to find out that Albert Romanstine was one of the smartest men I ever knew. No matter what the subject, he knew something about it. I never knew exactly how much schooling he had, but he read all of the time. Even by the campfire light. Albert was from central Texas. His parents had come over from Germany and settled in one of Stephen Austin's colonies down on the Guadalupe River back in the '50s. Albert was born there. This was his fifth cattle drive.

Porter spoke, "Listen up men. There's a herd bedded down just across the river. They came through yesterday and went on across. We'll go to the east of them, then straight north to Mud Creek. Their trail boss said they were going to rest the herd today, so we'll have to go around them. Once we get to Mud Creek, we'll stay on this side of the creek and follow it northwest. Cory, don't let any steers get past you. Each one is worth a month's wages when we get to Dodge City. Albert will take the point. I'll work the left side with Cory and Charley. The river crossing is fairly wide here. We'll let the steers get a good long drink and push them across real easy like."

I mounted up on the paint and we started moving around the herd. The cattle got lazily to their feet. I spotted the steer that I had had the fight with the day before. "No shenanigans today buster. Let's go." And believe it or not, that steer gave me that funny look again, like 'don't hit me again!' He turned and trotted to the head of the line like he knew where we were going and he was going to lead the way.

"I'll be dad-blamed," said the one called Charley. "We've been calling that steer Homer for the past four weeks because every day, and I mean every day, he tries to head back for home. And now he must think he's the lead steer. You educated that ornery cuss, Cory! Yeah boy. Be interesting to see if it lasts."

I found out later that Charley Opperude's family had come from Norway. He was the most laidback fellow I ever met. Always had a smile on his face. Charley once told me his family had settled in the Dakota Territory about 15 miles south of Canada. A couple of winters there was enough for him. The snow would be as deep as the edge of the roof of the house and a body had to tunnel out to get to the road. He told me once that all of the doors in the house opened inward, otherwise the deep snows could trap them inside the house. As soon as he was old enough, he drifted south to warmer weather and ended up in Texas.

One of Charley's jobs was to count the steers every morning to make sure a bunch hadn't wandered off or been stolen during the dark of the night. I soon found out that if some were missing we'd have to go looking for them before we could get started. Some days might take several hours tracking them down and catching them back up to the herd. Some days we'd never find one or two. Some days we'd find a few more than we had lost. If we found some unbranded, we'd rope, throw and brand them with a herd brand, and then take them along with us. If they had a brand, we'd take them along as well in case we met up with the herd that lost them. If we never did, we'd sell them along with ours.

"How do you count all these critters, Charley? They're all movin', and changin' places. It's seems impossible."

"It's easy as pie, young Cory. I just get down low to the ground, count all the legs and divide by four. Yeah boy!"

We weren't very far from the river. I could see why the other herd had gone across. They didn't want their steers to mix with ours. We moved out at an easy walk. The water in the channel was about 30 yards across with easy slopes on each side. To the east, the banks rose fairly high on the south side. To the west was Salt Creek on the south side and Red Creek over on the north side. The bank rose high on the north side just west of Red Creek. Red River Station was the crossing point for herds going up the Chisholm Trail. Just to the west of it, the river took a big turn going straight north and then east. It was running pretty much east and west where we crossed. Albert said the bottom here at the crossing was fairly solid due to the big turn in the river. Somehow it kept quicksand from forming here.

Red River Station was the main crossing for the Chisholm Trail because it had a good solid bottom and the gentle slopes on either side made it easy for the cattle. I took the paint to the flats just south of the water and waited there. Charley was doing the same on the north side. I watched him ride across – I had never crossed a river before. It wasn't really very deep. I saw him hold his stirrups up out of the water and he didn't get wet at all. I had heard that river crossings on the trail could be dangerous, but this one didn't look so bad.

The sun was just peeking over the horizon when the cows started across. It being near the Spring Equinox, it was about 7:30 in the morning when we got underway. I didn't own a watch but when you spend most of your life outdoors, you can tell time fairly well just by the sun up in the sky. A few steers started to come my way, but I shouted and waved my hat at them and they turned back to follow the others. I was watching Charley and he wasn't having any trouble either.

All of a sudden, I got a bad feeling. All of the cattle had different brands. Had I just signed on with a bunch of rustlers? Criminy! What do I do now? As I sat there, I got to thinking about the men I had met. All had been very friendly and not too rough looking. None of them fit any description of what I thought an outlaw would look like.

After about an hour, Porter rode up from the north side of the river and motioned me across. I turned the paint toward the river but when we got to the water, he balked. "Come on boy. You can do this. It's just a little water." Nope, not gonna do it, was the paint's reaction. Well, I couldn't just sit there and let the herd go to Kansas without us. With a big whoop and a holler, I gave that paint a big kick in the flanks and he bolted into the water causing a big splash and soaking me good. And I'm here to tell you that it can be quite chilly, and I mean downright cold, on a brisk early morning in early March. Brrrrrrr! I was colder than the bottom of the icehouse. Nothing I can do about it now but just grin and bear it.

Porter rode up and with a big grin said, "Cory, did you decide to get your Saturday bath in already?"

I was too cold to respond and I didn't want to risk Porter hearing my teeth chatter, so I just nodded.

"Head over to the supply wagon when it gets over there and change your clothes. Tell Hollis to give you Sandy's spurs. The paint and your other mounts will understand you a little better."

We had two wagons with our herd. One was the chuck wagon which Cookie drove. The other was the supply wagon which carried extra provisions, supplies and everyone's bedrolls and extra gear. Hollis drove it. He also helped the wrangler with the remuda. Hollis was a nice guy and would do anything for you, but he was a little slow in everything he did, said and understood. I rode over to the supply wagon as it rolled in from the east. They had crossed the River on the Spanish Fort ferry.

"Hollis, are there ferry crossings at all the rivers we'll cross?"

"There are on the big rivers due to the stage coaches and freight wagons needing to cross. But Cory, these wagons will actually float if the water gets too deep. It's a weird feeling when the mules are going one way and the wagon starts floating another way," Hollis explained, "but we use the ferries whenever we can since it is safer. Once the wagon starts floatin', it can just keep a goin' or tip over in the river. Then all your supplies are heading downstream!"

I dug my bedroll out and quickly put on dry clothes.

"Here, Cory, I'll string a line inside the wagon for you to hang your wet clothes on. Give them to me and I'll hang them up."

"Porter said for me to get Sandy's spurs."

"Yeah, he won't be needing them. He was always hot to trot. Argue about anything. Always thought he was right about everything. Treated me like I was stupid or somethin'. Said I didn't have anythin' north of my ears. Porter said you could have his gear if you needed any of it. He was about your size but bigger around."

I was stunned. Here was a better bedroll than my little army blanket and some extra clothes. I pulled out the spurs and put them on. "I'd better get back to the herd. Thanks a bunch, Hollis!"

"Don't mention it."

We walked the herd almost casually a few miles straight north. I thought we would go faster. So, this was Indian Territory. I didn't see any Indians. None of the guys seemed especially concerned that we could be attacked and scalped just any minute. Albert told me later that this area was part of the Chickasaw Indian reservation. The government set aside this Territory for all the Five Civilized Tribes that were to be relocated from their original homelands east of the Mississippi River.

Each tribe was called a nation by the government, so Indian Territory was also referred to as the Nations. The Choctaw Indians came to Indian Territory in 1832 and had all of the land in Indian Territory, south of the Canadian River from Arkansas to Texas. The Chickasaws were originally from Mississippi and came to Indian Territory in 1837. They had been friends with the Choctaws and the Choctaws welcomed them to come share their western lands in Indian Territory. The Chickasaws found out later, they were now the buffer between the Choctaws to the east and the fierce plains tribes to the west who raided them frequently.

The wealthier Choctaw and Chickasaw families had come first with their slaves and set up their large estates and ranches. The poorer ones were forced by the government to come later. Since the tribes had sided with the Confederacy during the War, the Choctaws and Chickasaws (and all of the Five Civilized Tribes) were forced to cede all of their lands west of the 98th Meridian. After 1866, the lands in Indian Territory west of the 98th Meridian were used for settlement of the plains Indian tribes.

This was pretty good land, not like the rocky hills near Liberty Chapel. Lots of grass. Rolling hills. It would make a nice farm and ranch someday. I heard one of the hands say that you could actually rent land from the Chickasaws.

At Mud Creek, we turned northwest and followed along the south side for just a few miles. It was almost noon. We had crossed several places where there were deep wagon ruts. Once the ruts got too deep for the wagons, the wagons just moved over a little. There were places where it looked like there were 4-5 sets of wagon ruts running side by side.

Around noontime, Charley and the other swingman, got in front of the lead steers and turned the herd into itself to stop them and let them graze. I could see the other herd when we passed it. It was about a mile away to the south. Charley rode by and said, "Let's eat! Yeah boy!" We rode together to the chuckwagon where Cookie had sandwiches and coffee ready for everyone. I got me a cup to get some water to drink out of Mud Creek, which wasn't all that muddy. Maybe it was after it rained.

Albert came by, "Cory, when you're finished, we'll go patrol the other side of the creek to make sure none of our critters wander off while we're here."

I switched my saddle to the sorrel I decided to call Socks and rode with Albert to the other side of the creek. None of the cattle crossed the creek. Actually, only a few of them went over to the creek for a drink and then walked back to the herd. Albert said they usually drank in the mornings and then again in the evenings unless it was hot. There had been a brisk breeze from the north which the trees along the creek had blocked somewhat during the morning. Riding the banks of the north side with Albert had no such protection and it was downright cold. Once we got the herd moving, Albert rode alongside for a while. I asked him, "why are we heading northwest instead of due north? Doesn't the trail go due north?"

"That's a good question, Cory. You see, we're crossing Indian lands and the Indians will want to charge us a toll for passing through. It's usually 40¢ a head per tribe. That's a lot of money when you figure we have over 2,400 head of steers and several reservations to pass through. Anyhow, the border between the Chickasaws and the Comanches is not too far west of here. There's no fences, signs or anything else to mark exactly where that border is, so Porter figures to go straight up the 98th Meridian – that divides the eastern tribes like the Chickasaws from the plains Indians like the Comanches, Kiowas, Apaches, Cheyennes and Arapahos. If we meet up with some Chickasaws that want money, Porter will try to convince them we're actually on the Comanche side. I doubt that will really happen as the Chickasaws don't want to be anywhere close to the Comanches. They're farming Indians and usually stay on the east side of the Cross Timbers. It's the plains Indians we have to worry about. Those tribes have only been on their reservations for about three or four years and still would rather fight anyone but their friends and allies. Sometimes if a toll is not paid, the Injuns will try to stampede the cattle in order to cut a few head out for themselves."

"If we happen to meet up with any Comanches, Kiowas or Apaches, Porter will tell them we're on the Chickasaw reservation. Who knows what any of them will do? We may have to fight them or keep them from stampeding the cattle so keep a sharp lookout. Porter will be roaming around and will know if there are any Indians about."

That evening, when I got off my pony and started to walk, my legs felt like I could stick a parasol through them and not touch either side. I felt like I was waddling when I walked. I had ridden horses before, but not all day long. This was going to take some getting used to. With the sun going down, it was definitely getting colder. I'll be sleeping outside from now on and I was glad for the extra clothes from Sandy.

As I was eating my beans, bacon, biscuits and bacon gravy, Porter came over to me and said, "Cory, since you're new, fresh and not too tired yet, you can take first watch on the nightshift – four hours, eight to midnight. Saddle up a fresh pony and just circle the herd slowly to keep a watch over things. Someone will relieve you at midnight. If you have any trouble, just take care of it. If you need us to come a runnin' just start hollering. Sound will carry almost a mile out here on the prairie. Whatever you do, don't spook the herd or they will stampede." Porter paused, "And that's a bad thing. Charley will be nighthawking too. You both will ride in opposite directions and meet up twice each time around. Any questions?"

"No sir."

I'd heard about stampedes and was determined not to be the cause of one. I saddled up the black and decided to call him 'Star'. The moon was just peakin' up over the horizon. Well a sliver of it anyway. There were some low clouds and as the moon rose, it peaked in and out of the clouds, but I could really see fairly well. I had learned never to stare at the campfire as it took quite a while for my eyes to adjust to the dark, so I was ready to head out.

The north wind was relatively slight, but still chilled my hands especially. Most of the cattle had bedded down and were chewing their cuds. Cattle were herd animals, meaning they didn't like to be alone, so they tended to stay together. The next four hours were uneventful and I actually liked it – being alone, not worrying about steers bolting for home. I had survived my first day on the drive. The days were going to be long, but that's OK. I can handle it.

The Chisholm Trail
Wednesday, March 3, 1880

The next morning, I had a hard time getting up. I had gotten to bed around midnight and it was now about six – an hour or so before sunrise. And I was stiff and sore. Oh, and how I ached all over! The bedroll I had inherited from Sandy was a large piece of canvas with a couple of blankets that I could roll up in. If there was to be rain or dew, I could spread the slicker I also inherited from Sandy to stay dry, or I could try to bed down under a wagon if there was room. I used my saddle as a pillow. Since it was so chilly, I had slept in my clothes only taking off my boots. I had bought them after Christmas at Justin's when he had a sale. They had the high heels that cowboys wore to keep their feet from going through the stirrups and possibly getting dragged to death if thrown off their pony. Of course, at the time that wasn't the reason I purchased this style. It was because the higher heels made me taller.

I rolled up the bedding I had inherited from Sandy and put it in the supply wagon. Getting a cup from the chuckwagon, I walked down to the creek for a nature break and to get some water. Back at the chuckwagon, Cookie was frying up the eggs he had gotten in Spanish Fort along with some ham and biscuits. Afterward, I walked back down to the creek for another drink and then it was time to saddle the palomino I decided to call Nellie.

As we got the herd moving, Albert rode up, "Cory, you take left flank again today and consider it your position from now on unless you're told otherwise. You're doing a fine job. Just keep the steers moving, give Harley a hand if he needs one, and don't let any of them run off. Got it?"
"Got it!"

We were still heading northwest so I asked Albert, "Why are we going to Dodge City anyway? Isn't it like 400 miles from here? I thought Abilene was closer."

"Young pup, just full of questions. That's a good thing. That's how you learn things – by asking questions. First question first. We kinda just mosey the steers up the trail. The fatter they are and the better shape they're in when we get to Kansas, the more money Porter can get for them. So we walk 'em slow, let them graze on the way and then at midday let them rest and graze for a couple of hours. Then it's back on the trail until sundown. We'll cross a lot of creeks and rivers so water is no problem. This time of year, there's 12 hours of daylight, so they're walking about 8 or 9 hours a day. We average about 8 – 12 miles a day. You'll see that it's not just a trail we're following. It's actually a very wide open prairie. Herds can't just follow each other since the herd in front would eat all of the grass. So they kinda go side by side. That's another reason why we go this time of year – when the grass is just starting to green up. If we went earlier, there wouldn't be any good grass, plus we'd all freeze to death, especially if a big norther came blowing in. If we went later, there wouldn't be any grass because previous herds may have eaten it down and it wouldn't have had time to grow back. Then once July comes, the spring grasses brown up and you have to rely on just the summer grasses for protein for the cattle. Grass only has protein in it if it's green. Plus in the summer, it's awfully hot and heat is hard on cattle, the ponies and the men. Look around you here, there's little bluestem and gramma grass. Just what you need for fat steers. We're just on the edge of the tall grass prairie where the big bluestem will grow as tall as you are. We may see some of it. Maybe not, since it is still early in the year."
"That makes sense, but why go to Dodge City? Isn't Abilene closer?"

"You know your geography, kid. Yes, Abilene is closer and Wichita is even closer. They are actually due north of here. But the State of Kansas won't let us go there or anywhere in the east half of Kansas anymore. You see, some of these Texas longhorns carry a tick that doesn't really bother them all that much, but causes a fever in domestic cattle like shorthorns. The cattle drives started right before the War by going up the Shawnee Trail over in the east side of the Nations to Sedalia, Missouri – the end of the railroad line at that time. When the Missourians' cattle started getting sick and they discovered it was from the longhorns. Missouri said, 'No more Texas cattle allowed in Missouri!' As the railroad got into eastern Kansas, the drives started going there, but then they wouldn't allow the longhorns with the ticks either. By about '67, the railroad had gotten west to Abilene where there wasn't much settlement, so the cattle started being herded there.

Soon the railroads started coming south to Newton and then to Wichita making the drives a little shorter. The railroad soon reached Ellsworth, which is west of Abilene. Herds kept going to all four towns depending on where the trail bosses thought they could get the best prices. But in '76, due to settlers moving west, the great state of Kansas drew a line on a map and said, 'no more Texas cattle east of this line!' That line was west of Abilene, Ellsworth, Newton and Wichita putting those towns out of the cattle business. By now the railroad had pushed on to Dodge City and that's where we all have to go now. Although I hear the railroad is pushing on south of Wichita to Caldwell and Kansas will allow herds to go there, it being just over the border from the Nations. But it'll be another year or so before it's finished. Since we started in eastern and south central Texas, we go up the Chisholm Trail like many herds have before us, but once we cross the Cimarron, we'll turn northwest on the Cimarron Cutoff and follow it almost to

Dodge City. Maybe next year's herds will go back up the Chisholm Trail like they used to – at least to Caldwell."
"Isn't there a trail that goes through the west side of Indian Territory to Dodge City?"

"Yeah, that's the Western or Great Western Trail. That trail crosses the main channel of the Red River at Doan's Crossing over in Greer County, Texas and doesn't get into the Territory until it crosses the North Fork of the Red. Texas says the North Fork is the boundary between Texas and the Territory, not the main channel."

"OK, I have one last question for you and I hope you're not offended."

"Never hurts to ask, son."

"OK, here goes – are these cattle stolen? They all have different brands. Have I thrown in with a bunch of rustlers?"

Albert threw back his head and laughed and laughed and laughed. "No, son, we're not rustlers – not yet anyway. We gathered these steers from various ranches down in Texas. Back in the old days, the longhorns were wild and ran loose because everybody was off fightin' in the War. All a body had to do was to hire a few hands, round up these wild critters, slap a brand on them and herd them up the trails to the railroads for big money. Nowadays, there are established ranches that raise these cattle. Most ranches aren't big enough to make up their own herd. It's more profitable for a drive to have 2,000 – 3,000 in a herd. So the ranchers entrust their cattle to someone like Porter. He goes around to the various ranches and picks up 200 head from this one, 400 head from that one, and so on until he has enough for a drive. That's why there are various brands. Porter keeps a tally book that has the number of

49

steers we've picked up at each ranch so he'll know how much money to take back to them. Along the way we may lose a few or pick up a few strays that are unbranded or lost from another herd. We brand all the cattle with a herd brand. If we lose some rancher's steers, those mavericks will make up the difference. If we have steers from another herd, we turn them over to them if we ever meet up with them. If we don't we just sell them with the rest of the herd. If there are any extra head left over from Porter's tally book, that money is divided up among the hands. Even if we lose some steers along the way, Porter wants to bring back money for every steer he took from a ranch. He's got a good reputation because of that. Other drovers keep the money from the mavericks and the ranchers take the loss for lost stock. If you'll notice, on the left shoulder of all of the cattle, there is a herd brand in case we get them mixed up with another herd. It's the Rockin' P. I'd better get goin' and show ol' Homer which way to Dodge City," and Albert trotted on up ahead.

The north breeze had subsided somewhat during the night and I had been very warm snuggled down in my bedroll. Now the breeze was picking up as the sun rose. The steers walked about 2-3 abreast and the herd strung out for quite a ways. We were traveling through shallow rolling hills, but the cattle did not walk in a straight line. They moved like a long serpent going around the hills and trying to stay on as level ground as they could. I rode up the hills and maybe 30 yards off. They all seemed to know what was expected of them for the day and I had no trouble keeping them going and together.

At the noon break, I switched my saddle back to Paint and we started the herd moving again about 2 o'clock in the afternoon. We walked them until almost sundown, when we circled them up again. They had been on the trail for over a month, so by now, they all knew their day was done.

Some lay down immediately planning to graze some during the night. Others seemed to just want to eat all of the time. We were still following Mud Creek, so we allowed the cattle access to the creek for an evening drink after a long day. Cookie and Hollis had driven on up ahead of the herd and knew where Porter was going to stop for the night. Cookie had his ovens going and hot biscuits were the highlight of the meal of beans, bacon and gravy. I ate quickly and crawled into my bedroll as I had second shift – from midnight to four am – to nighthawk.

Thursday, March 4, 1880

My first two days in Indian Territory were rather uneventful, which I felt was a good thing. Right near sundown each evening, the coyotes would start in yipping and howling. There always seemed to be several bunches around us in all directions. It sounded like they were singing and getting ready for a busy night. The steers didn't seem to pay much attention to them. I rarely saw a coyote out during the daytime.

My inner thighs were real sore from riding all day every day and part of the night. We hadn't seen any Indians although we really hadn't gone very far into the Territory. Breakfast that morning was good and hardy. There was still a chill in the air. Cookie had made bread and produced some apple butter to go along with the last of the eggs and some ham. I'm sure we had the eggs the first few days out as they probably wouldn't last long in the bouncing wagon. But boy, I could live on that apple butter! He must of picked that up in Spanish Fort as well, as that was the one and only time we had any.

We worked our way northwestward keeping just south of Mud Creek with me on the left flank as usual. Albert thought we were real close to the 98th Meridian, which was the western border of the 'Nations' and almost to the Comanche Indian reservation. The cattle stayed down off the hills as much as possible walking on fairly level ground. Only going up and down the hills when they had to. Otherwise they preferred to go around them.

The wagons stayed up on the ridges so they wouldn't bog down if the ground became soft. Where the water ran or gathered at the bottom of the rolling hills, the ground might be soft. I noticed several buffalo wallows up on these ridges from time to time. This is where the buffalo would roll on their backs and give themselves a dust bath, probably to help with flies.

There was another herd about a day ahead of us and probably a mile east of where we were traveling. We crossed their trail the day before. The prairie was all chewed up from the hooves of some 2-3,000 animals. Albert told me that Porter never got in a hurry with his herds. Some drovers thought that if they were the first herd to get to Dodge City they would get the best prices, but Porter said that the buyers knew other herds would be coming and the fattest herds in the best shape got the highest prices. So we just moseyed along making 8-12 miles a day.

Homer still trotted out to lead the herd every morning. Albert and Charley said I needed to slug all of the steers so they would follow Homer meekly and we could just ride alongside without much effort. However, that wasn't going to happen, and one little steer decided to take it upon himself to replace Homer in the dash for home. Every day after we had been on the trail for a couple of hours, this little steer would take off when he thought I wasn't looking. Today I was riding Nellie. She reared and spun around on her hind legs and with a jump was off after that steer when he took off. After a hard chase of a couple hundred yards, we got him turned around and headed back to the herd. I looked quickly around to see if any other steers had bolted, but didn't see any. This little steer made a habit of this just like clockwork. Once in the morning and sometimes in the afternoon. I started looking for a big stick. After a few days of this, I started calling the steer Homer, Jr or just Junior. I soon was ready to shoot him.

In the afternoon we traveled far, for the terrain was rolling prairie with only a few trees in sight – mainly here and there along a creek. We had left the mesquite and live oaks of Texas behind and saw some elm trees, cottonwoods, willow, and hackberry trees. But, like I said, there weren't very many trees at all. I saw no sign of Indians or that anyone had ever come this way, although I'm sure previous herds had in the last nine years the Chisholm Trail had been in use. I did see where there had been a prairie fire, probably back a month or so ago. It had been a mile or more wide and went from southwest to northeast, or vice versa. Most likely the wind had been blowing from the southwest. I couldn't really tell. As we crossed the blackened area, new shoots of green grass were already starting to grow. This is when grass is the most tender, plus it wasn't surrounded by the dead grass of last year. We had a hard time keeping the cattle moving through there. All they wanted to do was eat that new tender grass.

I rode back and forth some, between the rear end of the herd to about halfway up to the front. Sometimes I would have to push the steers that wanted to stop to eat. Most of the time I would just walk along about halfway and about 30 – 50 yards off. I kept a sharp lookout to the south and west of me for Comanches.

Nearing sundown, we topped a rise over a little valley with a little nameless creek at the bottom. Albert said it ran into Beaver Creek which was a few miles to the west. Beaver Creek ran into the Red River west of Red River Station. We had made about 14 miles that day. It had been a real nice day. Fairly warm. There were trees all along this creek with a high hill off to the northeast. There was easy access for all of the cattle to get to water without them having to spread out too far. After we had bedded the herd down, I rode over to the top of that hill. I bet I could see for 12 miles. I thought I could make out four other herds. One was way ahead of us to the northeast, another was about a mile away due east, another east and north of

54

them, and one southeast of us several miles. Wow, 10,000 head of cattle! More than I had ever seen. This little valley and the land stretching out to the east had the best grass I had seen since leaving Texas. It would make a nice homestead for someone if the Indians ever gave it up. We made camp here and bedded down the herd just below the top of the rise and south of the little nameless creek. It had good water in it. There were two sets of wagon ruts coming down the hill.

Since I had ridden nighthawk the past two nights, I wasn't called on tonight. I was a little disappointed. I liked the solitude and quiet of the night. The sunset was real pretty – all pinks and oranges with radiating sunbeams. I don't remember seeing that many amongst the scrub oaks around Liberty Chapel.

Friday, March 5, 1880

By now, everything was getting to be routine. My inexperience was wearing off. I had a good idea now of what I was expected to do and when to do it, so Albert and Porter rarely had to tell me anymore. The meals were getting kind of boring and seemed to be just the same thing all the time. Cookie frequently told the men to quit their belly aching. I guess there is just so much variety a chuckwagon can offer.

Charley was going on and on about itching all over. Seems like the chiggers had decided that he was the tastiest of us all. I never got too many chigger bites, but Charley seemed to be scratching all of the time. Must have been that pale Norwegian skin that the chiggers liked so much.

I enjoyed seeing the sunrise every morning and hearing the birds calling. I saw a bobcat down by the creek this morning. He could hear those birds too, except he was thinking breakfast!

Riding Socks this morning we jumped a jack rabbit. Socks took this opportunity to crow hop and buck a little bit although I'm sure he knew that jack rabbit was in the grass in front of us well before it took off.

I also saw some deer off in the distance. They didn't seem too concerned with us. I could hear quail and meadowlarks calling each other all throughout the day long.

Around dusk, I could hear the nighthawks 'swooshing' high in the air above.

One thing I noticed especially nighthawking around the little hills, was that down in the little 'valleys', the air seemed just a little bit colder. So in the evening, the question became – do I sleep up higher on a hill where I am most likely to be in the wind? Or do I sleep down lower where it might be colder? It had been so dry these past few months and even now, there wasn't any dew to get me and all my gear wet during the night. Or if there was some dew, the wind kept it off. I decided early on, that sleeping out of the wind was best. My blankets in the canvas bedroll kept me plenty warm. I laid an oil cloth on the cold ground for extra protection. The first decision of the evening was to determine which way the wind was blowing and bed down on the other side of a hill or in a buffalo wallow. However, some nights Mother Nature tricked me and the direction of the wind would change during the night. Although sleeping without my shirt and pants on was more comfortable, the discomfort of putting them on cold in the morning usually made me sleep with them on. I soon discovered I could take my shirt and pants off, and put them between my blankets and the canvas bedroll on top of me, keeping them relatively warm. Fortunately, the days were starting to warm up.

The coyotes were exceptionally loud tonight. Maybe they were on the trail of Mr. Jack Rabbit. The moon is getting brighter each night although it is rising later and later.

The sunset was a spectacular red again tonight. It looked like the clouds were on fire.

Saturday, March 6, 1880

There were ten of us drovers – two on point near the front on either side guiding the herd, two on swing (one on each side from the front to halfway back), two on the flanks (from halfway back to the rear on either side), and one, Harley, on drag (bringing up the rear), plus there were Cookie and Hollis who drove the wagons, the pony wrangler Matthew, who was responsible for everyone's ponies and, of course, Porter. Albert usually rode around to check on everything and everyone after we got started, then rode one of the point positions. We were a man short, so there were no days off and no getting sick. Sometimes the men would rotate around to other positions just to do something different.

Since I was the youngest and least experienced, I should have been riding drag, keeping the stragglers moving and eating the dust at the back of the herd. However, there was an older cowboy, Harley, who always rode drag. Porter had said he had been on many cattle drives and didn't much like to get out of a walk nowadays. A trotting horse was not to his liking. Once the cattle got moving and Albert had checked the men, the cattle and the ponies, he would sometimes ride out to meet with Porter or to go study the terrain in front of us to determine which way to tell the point riders where to lead the herd. Homer was now always the first steer in the line and leading all of the others. Behind him the steers walked 2-3 abreast, then 4-5 abreast, then sometimes more depending on how level the trail was in width. There were always the ones at the end that were either weak or lazy and weren't at all interested in keeping up with the others.

As time went by, I noticed the cattle all had different personalities just like the ponies. Some were leaders, some were followers. Some were mean, some had a gentle nature. And some were just plain trouble like Homer, Jr. and his buddies. They were always scheming a break for freedom little knowing that if they broke free of the herd never to be found, that they would end up as some Indian's supper and miss out on a train ride to Chicago.

A time or two over the past few days, I had ridden back to help Harley with the stragglers. I wasn't used to riding in all that dust. It was still fairly dry. The area hadn't had any rain in quite some time. The dust made me sneeze. Always twice at a time. I don't think that ever in my life I have ever sneezed just once. It's always twice. And I sneeze real loud. I think I have this unconscious sense of sneezing from the bottom of my lungs, whatever it is that is making me sneeze. Anyhow, it's a bad thing and a good thing. It's bad to be eating that dust which is making me sneeze, but my sneezes are so loud, it scares the lazy steers at the tail end of the herd and they'll trot off to catch up with the rest of the steers.

When all of the steers are being good and following the steers in front of them, I can hook one leg over the saddlehorn and just mosey along with them, half asleep in the saddle. You might have noticed that I always refer to the cattle as steers. We probably have just as many heifers as we do steers. The animals in our herd are around two years old and almost grown. The bull calves were cut when they were branded on a roundup as small calves so their meat would be more tender when they were big enough to be butchered. The heifers just had to be branded. Now they are all on their way to market.

During the times I can take a good look around especially when topping the hilltops, I notice there are a lot of hawks. I bet I saw one about every mile or even less. I don't remember seeing that many around home. Most of them had white bellies and their tails were red. They were about a foot tall maybe. I would see them high in the few trees along the creeks and out over the prairie they would just float up in the sky. There was one type of hawk. It was bluish looking with a white belly that seemed to soar just a few feet above the ground, dipping, turning, and circling, looking for rodents. Albert said that most of them winter down this far south and will head north when it gets warmer.

There were always buzzards circling high in the sky like they were just waiting for something to die. Sometimes one or two. Sometimes twenty.

Today was another nice day. The weather is fairly warm during the day after the chill burns off. It's chilly at night, but I seem to sleep better in the warm covers on a chilly night. I am having a hard time keeping my ears and hands warm during nighthawking though.

Sunday, March 7, 1880

I was the first one up. Streaks of light were just peeping over the horizon. Over here in the Territory or Nations, the rolling prairie stretches on and on (I kinda got the idea that only the eastern side of Indian Territory was referred to as the Nations). If you were to sit on a hill, I bet you could see for half a dozen miles. There was a chill in the air and the stars were still thick in the western sky.

I had slept in my clothes again to keep from having to put on cold clothes. I stowed my bedroll in the supply wagon, caught up Nellie, saddled her and led her back to camp. I could hear meadowlarks and quail calling.

"What's up, Cory? Hollis asked from deep within his bedroll. "Where ya goin'?"

"It's time to be up and at 'em! I don't want to be late for work."

"Cory, it's Sunday. We don't drive the cows on Sunday."

Cookie had just stirred up the coals from last night's fire and put on a pot of coffee. "That's right, Cory. Porter's family came across the plains on the Oregon Trail back in the '50s. They noticed the wagon trains that rested on Sunday, made it to Oregon or California faster and in better shape than those who rolled every day. So, we rest, the cattle rest and everybody is fresh and rarin' to go come Monday."

I unsaddled Nellie, grabbed my bedroll from the supply wagon and crawled back in my blankets.

Sitting around that Sunday, I was able to meet the other guys on the drive. Several of them had purchased new boots at Justin's place there in Spanish Fort. I'll tell you more about some of them later on down the trail. For now, just let me say that Willie James was just plain mean. He constantly tormented Hollis. He was about 18 and also on his first cattle drive, but he had joined them at the start way down in Texas. He treated me like I didn't know squat. But then again, I didn't.

We took turns riding around the herd for about two hours each that Sunday making sure none of the cattle strayed or got across the creek, although we did let them have access to the water. The other herd had gone on north and was way east of us. Albert said there would be several herds in front, beside and behind us the whole way.

As I spread out my bedroll near Hollis that evening, Willie walked by, "Better sleep with one eye open tonight boys, we're in Injun country. They'll sneak in after dark, slit your throat and take your scalp, and no one will ever know they've been here until you don't get up in the morning!"

Hollis and I looked at each other and pulled the covers up over our heads.

A few hours later, there was a big ruckus and I thought the Indians were attacking. I rolled out of my bedroll and crouched down low trying to see what was going on in the moonlight. The first thought I had was that I had not cleaned my pistol before going to bed like Dave had told me to. What if I needed it now and it misfired or jammed? I saw men running, but it looked like our guys not Indians. I held my fire. I really hadn't even noticed the gun in my hand until then. Then I could hear Albert laughing and Cookie yellin' and cussin'. "Dadburned ring-tailed bandits!"

I ran over to the supply wagon in time to see two coons jump off the back and run toward the creek with Cookie hot on their tails. The coons had gotten into the supplies and made a big mess of everything. What they didn't tear up, they had crapped all over. And these were our extra supplies.

Hollis climbed quickly into the wagon to clean up the mess. Cookie was soon back from his unsuccessful coon chase, "Hollis, my boy, you've got to make sure the wagon is tied down tight so critters can't get in and get into everything."

Porter came up, "What's the damages, Cookie?"

"Not too bad, but they sure made a mess of things. We'll know better when it gits daylight, but I'm shore we'll have to stop for some provisions somewheres along the way."

"Alright, we'll take inventory before we get to Duncan's Station. We'll pass close by. It's about 30 miles north of here."

Willie came stalking by, "Hollis, you jasper, I swear you're so dumb, you don't know 'come here' from 'sic 'em'."

I was wide awake (I thought it had been Indians and I was a goner. Scared the you know what out of me). Since I was supposed to ride nighthawk from 4:00 am to dawn, I saddled up and went on out letting Charley come in an hour early.

The rest of the night was quiet and peaceful and, quite pleasant under the stars and moon, although it was still a bit chilly.

Monday, March 8, 1880

We had camped by a tree-lined little creek. When I woke up, I stowed my bedroll, got my cup, and went down to the creek for a nature break and for some water. As I approached the creek, I heard a rustling and froze. My first thought was Indians or some wild critter out for an early breakfast. On the other side of the creek in the faint light, I could make out a turkey walking by. Then another. And another. I counted 19 in all. I had never seen that many turkeys. I don't think they ever saw me.

As I've said before, the herds all moved north sometimes along the same trails, sometimes parallel to each other. All along the trail as we rode toward Dodge City, I could tell that our pathways had been used quite a bit before. In some places, grass had grown over the trail from the past year's drives. In others, the water from hard rains had eroded the trail into steep and narrow washes that were sometimes hard to travel. And there were usually wagon ruts paralleling the trail up on a ridgeline. The ground was firmer up there and not as soft where the wagons might bog down.

We had crossed a well worn road. No grass, all dirt. It was several wagons wide in places. This must be where the freight wagons and stagecoaches ran most of the year. I rode along the road for a ways just out of curiosity. Albert had told me earlier that freighters had used the trail for years before the cattle drives started. That made sense. I didn't know there was a road going through Indian Territory. I thought the Chisholm Trail was a trail for herding cattle. Here on the wide open prairie there were endless routes possible for miles. Over to the east was the impenetrable Cross Timbers. Over to the west was dry with short sometimes sparse grass and wild Indians.

It looked like when the ruts got too deep in one spot, the freighters just moved over a bit and made a new road as long as the terrain allowed for it. We were traveling several miles west of that road. I'm sure we didn't want the stagecoaches spooking the cattle as they went by hell bent for leather, plus we wanted to stay out where the grass had not been eaten or worn down.

We had two mules pulling each of our two wagons. I had always heard that mules were a lot better than horses at pulling wagons. I noticed there were six extra mules in with the remuda so they too could be swapped out each midday and be kept fresh for the long journey.

An animal always travels the road of least resistance. Therefore, you'll never see an animal travel in a straight line. Out here on the prairie it's obvious. The trails always look like they are meandering in a lazy fashion. Not in a big hurry. The truth is, a cow (or any animal traveling cross country) will always try to stay on as level ground as much as possible even if it means walking a longer distance. No walking up and down hills with extra effort, but going around if it gets them where they eventually want to end up. That makes sense. I've never saw any of the town's milk cows get in a hurry until they knew there was a feed bucket waiting for them.

I had always thought the Chisholm Trail was flat and broad and straight. Not so. It was rolling prairie most of the way with small hills and valleys, and miles wide to accommodate all of the thousands of cattle heading north to the railroad.

The Chisholm Trail was the perfect trail.

Comanches
Tuesday, March 9, 1880

We were up before daybreak today, eating breakfast as the sun rose. Like last night, this morning's sun gave quite a show illuminating the clouds with pinks, oranges and reds.

"Albert, are all sunrises on the prairie this pretty?"

"This time of year and in the Fall, Cory, I must say they are along with the sunsets. However, before too long they will lose their luster to you. There's an old saying, 'Red sky at night, sailors delight. Red sky at morning, sailors take warning.' "

I wasn't real sure what that meant.

I saddled my pony for the morning and headed out to the left flank position.

Then the wind started to blow. Up to now there had been a nice breeze each day. Now, it blew hard.

We got the herd started and headed them due north. Sure enough Junior took off after a couple of hours. This time it took me and Socks a quarter mile to catch up to him. We finally got behind him and got him turned around. The wind was biting and I had a hard time keeping my hands warm. That wind seemed to go right through me. I could tie my reins together and keep my hands in my coat pocket to keep them warm. Just walking along with the steers, I could guide Socks using my knees. But then a steer would break away or slow down and we'd have to push him back to the herd. Then I could only put one hand in one pocket until the other hand was too cold. Then I'd stick that hand in my pocket with my now warm hand on the reins.

Chasing Junior now, one hand was always frozen. I hated that steer.

The wind also made my nose drip. I was constantly putting one finger to the side of my nose to stop up one nostril so I could blow the snot out of the other side and vice versa. I didn't want to use my bandana cause I had no way of washing it. It was more for covering up my face on dusty days.

I got this weird feeling so I looked back over my shoulder to see three Indians sitting on their ponies up on a hill not 200 yards away. I hurried Junior back to the herd and was relieved to see they didn't follow me. I rode up to Charley who was riding swing in front of me and told him what I saw. I saw him ride up to the point to pass the information on to Albert. Nothing happened during the rest of the morning, but I noticed from time to time that the Indians were following us. They looked big and bulky sitting on their ponies. They must be wearing buffalo robes. I did discover later that wearing my slicker over my coat on those cold windy days helped. The wind couldn't get through it.

After the midday break, Albert came over to me and said, "Cory, ride point. Keep the herd due north. In a few miles, you'll see a tall hill, Lookout Hill, off in the distance. Aim for the west side of it. We should make that point by sundown."

Albert took my place on the left flank and kept an eye on the Indians. I wondered where Porter was and what he would do about them. After a few miles, I could see Lookout Hill off in the distance whenever we topped a hill, so I headed the cattle for it with Homer following close behind. Riding along and looking left and right for anything unusual, I spotted some animals off to the east, my right. Willie James was riding right swing. I rode over his way a little until I caught his attention and motioned him toward the animals. He rode over that way to investigate. He came back herding three steers all of them limping.

"Looks like they're lame, Cory, and couldn't keep up with their herd. Maybe we'll have some steak tonight!"

I thought about those Indians and had an idea, "Let's herd them along for a while. We might be able to use them later."

We bedded the herd down early that day, well before sundown. Porter must be expecting trouble. We were on the west side of Lookout Hill.

That night Porter doubled the nighthawks and we talked about the Indians and what to do if they attacked, which Porter didn't think they would. But they might be thinking about stampeding the herd so they could steal a few head during the confusion. The Comanches and Kiowas had only been on the reservation for four years and before that they had been raiding, murdering, scalping. Well you get the picture. I told Porter about the three crippled steers we had found a few hours ago, "Why don't we offer them to the Comanches and maybe they'll go away?"

Porter looked at me real funny, thought a few minutes and said, "That's a good idea, Cory." You can take the steers to them first thing in the morning." At first I thought he was kidding, but then I realized he wasn't.

Great. Since I'm the youngest, I guess I'm expendable. I was sure to be scalped tomorrow. So, it being my last night on Earth, I volunteered to ride nighthawk. I wouldn't be able to sleep anyway. I cleaned my pistol real good, then decided to ride up to the top of Lookout Hill before it got dark to take one last good look at the world. When I got to the top, I bet I could see for 20 miles to the west. To the east was another hill. I rode down and up over to the next high hill only to find a third hill. I rode over there as well and counted four herds off to the east. One about a day ahead of us to the northeast, one probably three miles to the east, another about a day behind us to the southeast and the other looked to be right behind us just coming over the horizon. I heard a noise and turned to see Porter riding up.

"Didja find a nice view, Cory?"

"Yes sir."

"There was a time not too many years ago, that you could count 20 herds from these hills. That's about 50,000 animals. Those herds were going to Abilene, then also to Newton and to Wichita. When the trains reached Dodge a lot of those herds went way west of here. Since the east Kansas markets were closed off to us, not too many herds go this way anymore. Maybe when the rails get to Caldwell, we'll be able to see more herds from here."

"Mr. Porter, why are we going this way instead of the Western Trail."

"Good question, Cory. Since we pick up most of our steers in eastern and south central Texas, it doesn't make sense for us to swing that far west. Plus with fewer herds going this way, the grass is usually better and the trail is not so crowded. And don't worry too much about tomorrow. You'll be just fine."

"What's that smell?"

"That would be Stinking Creek, right over there. It must have a little sulphur in it. Over there is the headwaters of Mud Creek. It's the one we followed those first couple of days after crossin' the Red."

There was another 'red sky' at sundown. I rode nighthawk again from eight to midnight and sure enough the wind didn't blow all night.

Comanches Up Close
Wednesday, March 10, 1880

The next morning I couldn't eat. I didn't sleep well. My stomach was in knots. My hands were actually shaking a little. I'm sure the sunrise was spectacular again but I didn't notice. I went off in the bushes to answer nature's call and it took a lot of leaves and grass to clean up. Washing my hands in the ice cold water in the creek just added to my misery.

Suffice it to say I was really nervous. I cleaned my pistol again even though I had cleaned it just the night before. I saddled up Nellie and got ready to ride when Porter came up behind me, "Cory, they're just out to the west. Herd the cattle slowly and deliberately right to them. Whatever you do, don't pull your gun unless they shoot first. I don't think they will. You'll just have to dodge that first shot. We don't want to start a war. Act like you do this all the time and it's no big deal. Don't let them think that you are scared."

I gathered the three crippled steers and pushed them to the northwest at a slow walk. After a few hundred yards, I turned to look back at the herd for the last time. Everyone was getting the herd moving and no one was looking my way. Well, that shows how much I rate!

Once again, I had gotten myself into a mess and I was determined to get through it somehow. I pushed those lame steers along, walking slowly. I didn't see any Indians. After half a mile, we topped a rise and there were the three Indians I had seen the other day sitting over on the next rise. I raised my arm in a half wave and drove the steers directly toward them. They didn't move or return my wave. As I rode near them, the only thing I could think of was how many people had each of them killed and scalped? I

71

just knew I would be the next one. I thought it best not to show how scared I really was and drove those steers almost right into their ponies.

I raised my hand again, "Do any of you speak English?" None of them said anything. They just stared unblinkingly at me. "These steers are for you."

"Why you give us?" asked the oldest looking one. I was glad to see that none of them were wearing any warpaint.

To get you to go away, I thought. "They are crippled and cannot keep up with the herd," I replied, "You can put them to good use. They will feed many families."

"You pay us to drive cattle on our land."

"Trail boss says we are on Chickasaw land," I replied. "We do not owe the Comanche anything. These are a gift."

"How come they send boy to bring cattle? Are the rest afraid?"

"It was my idea to give them to you."

"You are brave and now you are our friend."

With that they took the three steers and headed slowly back west over the hills. The youngest one was the only one to look back. I felt so weak I had a fear of falling off Nellie. I turned around and rode slowly back to the herd expecting to feel an arrow in the back at any moment. I hadn't even noticed how hard the wind was blowing. After I had ridden about 50 yards or so, Porter came up to me from the left and Albert from the right. They both had their rifles out.

"So you guys were watching"?

Porter grinned and said, "We weren't about to let you go it alone, old son. Al and me had Winchesters aimed right at them the whole time. We just thought you'd want to meet some Injuns up close and personal all private like."

"Thanks." But there were two of you and three of them, I thought. I still felt lucky to make it back to the herd in one piece. Junior must have known about the Indians because that day he never tried to run off. I guess he didn't want to be anybody's supper before he had to.

"Cory, you ride swing over on the other side. I reckon you've seen enough Injuns for one day."

I rode back and around the herd and up to the swing position. Lookout Hill was now about three miles behind us. The cattle were all moving well and seemed completely unaware of the morning's happenings.

I felt all morning like I was either going to throw up or freeze to death.

Duncan's Station
Thursday, March 11, 1880

We had made about 12 miles yesterday and were due north of Lookout Hill. Yesterday was fairly uneventful, except for it being so windy. I saw Junior take off twice and Willie chasing him down. I felt good just to be alive. The day before, I was sure yesterday was going to be my last.

At breakfast Porter came up to Hollis and me, "Boys, I want you to take the supply wagon and go to Duncan's Station for supplies. Cookie will give you a list. I'll ride over later and settle up with him. Ride north northwest for about eight miles. It's an old trading post on Cow Creek. You'll cross the stage road before you get there. Stay on it and it will take you straight to the post. When you're ready to head back, go straight east on the old military road to meet up with the herd. Any questions?"

"No sir," we both replied.

"Cory, do you have any money?"

"Yes, sir, I have $2.17."

"Here's an advance," and he handed me five dollars. Porter strode off and we were soon surrounded by all of the drovers. Each man wanting something from the Station.

"We better make a list." I got pencil and paper from Cookie and wrote down what they each wanted, tobacco and candy mostly, and how much money they gave Hollis. Matthew helped us catch the mules. We hitched up the team and prepared to move out.

"Boys, take this with you," as Albert handed up a rifle. It was a 1873 Winchester .44-40 repeating rifle, lever action and it was a beauty. It had a long barrel and was well balanced.

We took off across country excited to be on a mission and away from those noisy steers. Hollis drove and I rode shotgun with the rifle in my lap. The prairie was quiet except for the creaking wagon and rattle of the braces. There was not a cloud in the sky. Meadowlarks jumped up in front of us only to fly a few feet and land back down hidden in the grass.

The excitement of our mission soon wore off. I had no idea how rough it was riding in a wagon across the prairie. I had only ridden on established roads around home which were rough enough, but they were smooth compared to driving over the prairie. There were no roads out here where we were. We jostled, jolted, and lurched until my guts hurt. Hollis was obviously used to it as his body swayed with the wagon. About the only benefit to riding in the wagon was it got me out of that south wind – more or less.

We were about halfway there when we spotted two men on horseback heading our way. They weren't Indians and they didn't look like cowboys. I had a bad feeling about this.

"Howdy, boys! Where ya headin'?" asked the tall one. Both men looked a lot alike so I guessed they were brothers. The tall one looked to be the older of the two.

Papa always said, 'Never let 'em see you sweat.' That was going to be hard. They had ridden up on our left and I was sitting to the right of Hollis. I made sure the rifle laying across my lap was pointed right at them with my hand on the trigger. Problem was, I didn't remember if I had cocked it. A person didn't usually carry a rifle with a bullet in the chamber as it could go off accidently. So, I didn't think I had cocked it. Not good.

"We're with a herd on the way to Dodge City. We're heading to Duncan's Station for supplies," I replied. "My name's Cory. This is Hollis. What's yours?"

"Nosy little fella, aren't cha?" sneered the other brother.

"Just bein' friendly," I replied as I looked him right in the eye and slightly shifted the rifle just so he'd notice it.

The older brother laughed, "Well, we're friendly too, Cory. I'm Llewelyn and this is my brother, Charles. We're heading north looking for opportunity."

I wasn't sure what that meant but said, "Pleased to meet ya, Llewelyn and Charles." I had found that if I repeated someone's name that I just met, I could remember their name better. Otherwise, I sometimes didn't remember their name by the end of our conversation.

"You boys be careful. You never can tell when you might meet up with some outlaws or Injuns." The other brother snickered and they rode off in front of the wagon and off to our right over the prairie heading north.

We pulled into William Duncan's Station a couple of hours later. There wasn't much to it. There was a lady also working there that I took to be his wife. She looked like an Indian. We got out Cookie's list first and handed it to Duncan, "Mr. Duncan, this is for our supply wagon. Porter said he would be by later to settle up with you."

"Aye, would that be Robert Porter?"

Up until then, I hadn't known whether Porter was his first name or last name. I didn't even know if Robert was his first name. "Yep, that's him," replied Hollis.

"He's a good man, laddie. Been by here many times. I'll get started right on it."

"We also have a list for the men that we need to keep separate."

"No problem, lads. Here have a piece of candy while you wait and have a good look around. You may not know you need something until you lay eyes on it."

We walked around the store looking at all the stuff he had. I was going to get me some candy, but then I saw something I had to have – boxes of cartridges. I had yet to shoot my pistol and only had the 37 cartridges Dave had given me. I thought I better buy some .45's and practice a little.

When it was time to settle up with Duncan, I asked for two boxes of .45s. "Don't you want any candy, me boy?"

"I think learnin' to use my gun will be a better use of my money. We met a couple of guys on the trail that I don't think could be persuaded to leave us be if we offered them candy."

"Oh come now, lad? What did these two gents look like?"

We described them and then I said, "The tall one said his name was Llewelyn. The other one was Charles. They looked alike so may have been brothers."

Duncan laughed and slapped his thigh, "Lads, you met a couple of the Marlow brothers. Folks around here think they're bad eggs, but no one has ever caught them rustlin' or stealin' - yet. Be glad they decided not to rob you. They also have three younger brothers so it's best not to get any of them riled."

"Cory had them covered with his rifle and had them talkin' real friendly." Hollis said.

Duncan was still laughing, "Well, you lads have spunk. It's always good to try to make friends first and fight as a last resort. Let's see now, Charley owes 75¢, Albert owes $1.17, Willie owes 58¢" and on down the list he went. Hollis brought out a small sack with coins and bills. He handed it to me, "Cory, will you take this? I'm not too good at countin' money."

"Shore," I counted out the money for each man's purchases and made sure we got the right change.

We loaded the wagon with the supplies and got ready to head back to the herd.

"You boys in a hurry? There's a stage due around noon today. It's bound for Ft. Sill. There's always interesting folks on that stage. Maybe a colonel or even a general!"

"Thanks, Mr. Duncan, but we better get back."

We turned the wagon due east toward the herd. There was somewhat of a road that we could follow, so the ride wasn't as rough as coming in across the prairie. I found out later that it was a military road that went between Ft. Arbuckle to the east and Ft. Sill to the west. My back hurt from all the lurching and jolting coming in and, probably from loading the wagon. I had been sitting on a horse all day for the past ten days.

I found out later that Duncan had slipped a couple of pieces of hard candy into the sack with my two boxes of .45s along with the vest and canteen I bought (I was getting pretty tired of making so many trips to the creek with just a cup). I also needed the vest because I couldn't put anything in my back jeans pockets. It made for most uncomfortable sitting in the saddle all day. Most of the guys wore a vest mainly to have extra pockets. I didn't have any loops in my gunbelt so I needed some way to carry some extra cartridges. Plus it would help against the wind.

The herd had stopped for the midday break when we caught up to them. We handed out the tobacco, candy, razors, bandanas and so on. Then counted out the change to all the men. I saddled up Star and rode out to meet Bird who was circling around the herd. Now Bird was a strange one. I think he was Indian or part Indian. He rarely said a word and looked pretty wild. He had long black hair, black eyes and wore a buckskin shirt and moccasins. He usually sat apart from the other men. He was always riding into camp of an evening with a rabbit, turkey or deer to give to Cookie. I never saw him away from his post, but then I don't ever remember hearing any gunshots either. He had asked for a pair of socks and a bandana. No tobacco or candy. I gave him his stuff and a piece of candy that Duncan had given me.

Bird held up the candy between his thumb and forefinger and looked at me questionly. "It's some extra candy from the store. Thought you might like some," I said. I nodded at him and turned back toward the camp. When I looked back, he was still in the same spot and looking my way.

Hollis had told Albert about us meeting the Marlow brothers and Albert asked me a few questions, mainly what did they look like. I tried to describe them the best I could. Albert said, "I've heard of them, but have never run across them. I think they are fairly new in this part of the country. We'd better tell Porter and keep a close eye on the steers."

After supper, I could barely stand up straight. My back had really tightened up. I was to experience back spasms for a week before my back would loosen up. It was worse getting up and around after sitting or lying down, or getting off my pony. Once it loosened up, it wasn't too bad. Socks and I rode nighthawk that night. There was a cool breeze, but not too bad. It did seem to be warming up some. Hollis was riding nightherd on the remuda. I swung by to check on him every so often. He didn't like being out in the dark.

Rush Creek
Friday, March 12, 1880

Ugh, I could hardly stand up straight. It rained some during the night and I hadn't slept very well. I had to pull the canvas and my slicker over my face so I wasn't able to breathe in any fresh air. I needed a bath! My back hurt like the dickens. After some stretching and walking around it loosened up some. Standing still to eat breakfast, it tighten up again.

We crossed Wildhorse Creek about 9 o'clock that morning with no incidents except some rain which came and went. Not a real hard rain. Just enough to make you miserable with the cold wind. The site of the old abandoned Fort Arbuckle as about 40 miles downstream. After yesterday, I was hoping the cold weather was over.

Junior tried to run off once he got to the other side of the creek and thought he was hidden in some trees. I was riding left flank again and had to throw a rope on him. I was getting better with the rope. I dragged his butt back to the herd. OK, now how do I get the rope off of him? Maybe I hadn't thought this through. Thank goodness he wasn't ornery like Homer had been and his horns weren't very wide. Junior never acted like he was going to charge us or run over us. Him running off all the time seemed like it was just a game to him. I had looped the rope around his horns. I stopped when I got to the herd not knowing what to do next. Junior just walked on by like the game was over and he got caught. I was able to reach over and pull the lasso loose from around his horns. I needed to ask Albert how to unloose my lasso. I found out later that I needed to shake the noose bigger and bigger until it slipped over the steer's shoulders and he just kind of walked right out of it.

We crossed Rush Creek late that afternoon and bedded down the herd on the north side. The grass was all wet everywhere from the day's rain. I decided to put my bedroll under the supply wagon with Hollis in case it rained again tonight. I needed to breathe fresh air and no, I wasn't going to go take a bath in that ice cold creek water.

Cookie had set up camp by the springs where the water was fresh. There was plenty of trees nearby and Hollis was filling the canvases hanging under the wagons with firewood. I filled my new canteen with the cool spring water. I was getting used to being in the saddle all day and wasn't feeling so bow-legged any more.

As I lay there trying to fall asleep, I could hear a hoot owl near the spring. Another one answered back not too far down the creek. Sleeping outside on the prairie was actually quite noisy. Hoot owls, coyotes, tree frogs. All sorts of critters talking back and forth during the night. It was cowboy music. I hadn't really given that much thought.

I was a cowboy!

Little Washita River
Saturday, March 13, 1880

When I awoke, I peeked out from under the covers to find a tarantula crawling on me. I had seen them around our house in Liberty Chapel many times. I caught them and played with them as a boy knowing they weren't poisonous. Just scary looking. I slowly moved the covers and put my hand out flat, palm up, for the big spider to crawl onto. I could see that Willie hadn't moved yet so I snuck over, put the tarantula on him and snuck back into my bedroll. Cookie must have seen me as he started yelling for Willie to get up and get him some firewood. Willie pulled his covers from his face, saw that big spider and let out a loud scream. He was up and out of bed like a flash. I had to pull the covers down tight over my face so he wouldn't see me laughing. I peeked out and caught Cookie's eye which winked at me. Willie, we'll see who can scare who.

The sun was halfway up in the sky before you could see it over the clouds. Definitely lots of reds and pinks, so I knew it was going to be a windy day again. Sure enough, a couple hours after sunrise, there was a strong wind from the north with a bit of a bite to it. To this day, I don't know why the wind dies down around sundown and again around sunrise. It is a welcome relief though.

We made good time today. About 16 miles. The man that usually rode drag, Harley, was sick that day, so I had to watch half of the drag as well. Bird was riding the right flank and watched the other half. It took a lot of riding – twice of a normal day – going from the middle of the rear of the herd back around to the middle along the side, keeping those steers moving. Junior took off as always and by the time I got him back, the remuda was mixing with the slowpokes at the back of the herd. Bird and I got them separated without Matthew having to help us. I sneezed a couple of times and the steers ran up to join the others.

The problem with riding drag was the dust. The wind was blowing from the north and all the trail dust was blowing right into my face. Well, it seemed like all of it was blowing in my face and I was inhaling it all. I doubt if any of it got by me. No wonder Harley was sick. After a rain, it amazed me how fast the wind could dry everything out so quickly.

Like I've said before, if you ever hear anyone sneeze fairly loud and always twice, you know it's me. That dust would make me sneeze, two times every time, and every so often. The steers near me would jump and take off running. Luckily, the whole herd being strung out couldn't hear me sneeze, so there was no danger of a stampede, but I didn't have any trouble keeping the laggards up with the rest of the herd. I couldn't keep my nose from running due to the cold biting wind, and I couldn't keep from sneezing due to the all of the dust.

Harley rode drag most of the time due to his age. It was hard to tell just how old he was, but a walking pony was just his speed. One interesting thing about him was that he had taught his ponies to nip the steers on the top of their tails or on their flanks if they lagged too far behind. After a few nips, the steers would trot on ahead when they saw Harley coming. As we went farther up the Trail, other steers would start to get slower. They soon learned not to lag too far behind when Harley approached or they would be bit by Harley's ponies. Not sure what was wrong with Harley today, but I had heard him coughing most of the night. His lungs were probably full of dust.

Even after weeks on the trail, there were always a few steers that tried to sneak away, including Junior. I had a strange suspicion that he was organizing a few of his buddies to make a break for it with him soon.

After crossing the Little Washita late that evening, we bedded down the herd. There was good grass among the rolling hills to last a couple of days. As we approached the Washita River to the north, the country got more and more hilly. I'm hoping it will probably flatten out to a big wide plain like the crossing at Red River Station once we get nearer the river. Albert said the Washita was up due to some rains to the northwest. Our timing was good as tomorrow was Sunday and it would give the river some time to go down.

Kiowas
Sunday, March 14, 1880

I had ridden the late watch nighthawk on Nellie and didn't get back to camp until sunup. I found that I only needed about six hours sleep and could even doze a little in the saddle if my back didn't seize up. Cookie made us all flapjacks with lots of bacon. We had brought him some eggs from Duncan's Station.

I found a shade tree away from camp and laid down to get a couple more hours sleep. My plan today was to take my pistol out and practice shooting it. I had yet to shoot it at all although I had established the habit of wiping it clean every evening. I saddled Paint and Hollis got his pony. We told Cookie we were going to practice shooting a mile or so to the west so we wouldn't disturb the herd and headed off.

We found a good spot that was level for about 30 yards with a high bank behind it and out of the wind. We had brought some empty cans Cookie gave us and set them up on an old fallen log. Hollis stood behind me and held his hands over his ears – he didn't like loud noises.

I shot five rounds, switched out the cylinders and shot five more. Those 1858 Remingtons with the conversion cylinders only held five rounds. The smoke from the blackpowder was pretty thick, but, oh, how I love that smell. I switched cylinders, loaded the empty cylinder with five more shells, put it in the side holster and shot five more rounds. I got to where I could hit 3 or 4 of the cans with five rounds from about 15 - 20 yards consistently using both hands on the pistol. I remember Dave telling me to always keep a cylinder loaded, so I would reload the newly shot up cylinder immediately after putting the fresh cylinder in the pistol. I kept that extra cylinder always loaded on my gunbelt.

After I had shot about 30 rounds, I stopped to wipe out the cylinders and the revolver as that blackpowder was pretty messy and could affect the spin on the bullet. If the barrel of the gun wasn't clean, the bullet won't spin properly thus spoiling your aim. When the smoke cleared we noticed there were five Indians sitting on horses on a hill to our west. They looked different than the Comanches we had seen. They had war paint on and looked pretty mean and started heading our way. My gun was empty. It was time to see how fast I could switch cylinders, plus I only had five shots before having to switch cylinders again! We were in big trouble.

When they were about 30 yards away, they pulled up all of a sudden, turned and rode swiftly over the hill. We turned to see three horsemen riding hard in our direction. I thought it was some of the men from the herd so I just stood there. It wasn't. It was three of the Marlow brothers. "Well, well, well, if it's not our old friends, Cory – and Hollis wasn't it?" It was Lewellyn.

"Howdy, fellas. Nice of you boys to drop by just now," I replied as I tried to calmly reload my pistol. Hollis moved somewhat behind me. I knew none of the guys from the herd would show up to help us as they all knew we were out here target shooting and the gunshots would be expected.

"We heard the shots and thought we would come see what the ruckus was all about. Then we saw them Kiowas a-comin' at cha, so we stepped it up a little bit, in case they had a little mischief on their minds."

"Much obliged. Where y'all headin'?"

"Oh, just about anywhere opportunity knocks, my young friend Cory. Now you remember what I told you the other day about bein' on the watch for outlaws and Injuns."

"Yessir!"

"Adios" with a wave from Llewelyn, they rode back to the south. In a few minutes Albert came galloping up.

"I saw some men on horseback headed over this way. Are you boys alright?"

I told him about the Kiowas and how the Marlow brothers had ridden up just in time to save our scalps. "Maybe they're not such a bad bunch after all." The three of us headed back to camp. Hollis was pretty shaken after being so close to the Kiowas so I took his turn at watching the remuda that night, and then rode a two hour shift around the herd. It took me quite a while to get my revolver really clean from all that blackpowder.

Crossing the Washita River
Monday, March 15, 1880

The Washita River valley was several miles across and very flat. We passed a trading post off to the west. I think someone named Fred ran it, but since we wanted to get across the Washita before dark, no one went over there.

The wind was blowing fairly hard out of the southwest when I first smelled smoke. Looking back that direction, I saw a line of white and gray clouds stretching across the not too distant horizon. Fire! I pulled my pistol and fired into the air three times real fast. All of the men looked my way and saw the smoke barreling toward us. Pulling out our ropes we whipped the cattle into a frenzied run – they had just caught the smell of the smoke as well.

"Get 'em across the river!" I heard someone yell. I could see the flames of the prairie fire by now and it looked like it was on a course to cut us off before we got to the river. I bet those damned Kiowas set that fire.

The Washita River itself was different than the Red in that the river bed wasn't all that wide but the sides were very steep. We weren't going to be able to drive a lot of cattle across at the same time. At least the water level had gone down some from the day before, but the current was still running strong. We were looking at about a 30 - 40 yard swim. It felt a little warmer than yesterday. I was pushing the cattle from behind as Harley was still ailing and watching the left flank on the south side of the crossing. Lots of riding. I was riding Star today. Porter had found a good crossing with a rock bottom almost a mile to the east, so that gave us a little extra time. But there were only a half dozen trails leading down to the water. This was going to take forever!

Albert, and the two swing riders had their ropes out and were using them to whip the leaders down the embankment. We couldn't let them stop for a drink. Finally, Homer figured out what was wanted of him and he led the way. Albert was right with him and they both went into the current together. The rest of the herd followed.

The river was running fairly high and all of the men, ponies and steers climbed out on the far side about 100 yards east of where they went in, but there were good trails for climbing out there and the crossing was on. The channel wasn't as wide as the Red but the water was deeper. The steers sensed the urgency of the crossing and got across in record time. I got wet again, but it was a little bit warmer than last time – and no one got burned up in the fire. We had most of the herd across and now came the ponies. We helped Matthew and Hollis get the remuda across and took the opportunity to change to fresh ponies. Thankfully the river channel stopped the fire and we were safely on the other side.

During the crossing, Albert and the two swingmen continually rounded up the steers that had crossed so we could keep the herd bunched as the rest of them crossed. What they didn't notice was Junior and three of his pals had slunk off down the north side of the river to the west. Pushing the herd across from the rear and keeping the balking steers from turning back kept me from doing anything about it.

I got Paint and went after Junior and his bunch. They had about a two hour start. I rode along the north slope of the river and followed their trail west. I soon found where they had climbed out up the north bank and were trotting to the northwest alongside the river. I ought to just let them go and let them feed a bunch of wild Indians, I thought. But Porter's words of every steer was worth a month's wages, calculated to four months lost wages if I didn't bring them back.

There was a grove of cottonwood, elm and hackberry trees up ahead. When I topped the rise, Junior and his buddies spooked and headed right into them and into a mess of briers, locust and bois d'arc trees. Paint automatically went right in after them. The briers weren't very tall, but tugged at my boots and threatened to trip Paint. Those bois d'arcs and locust trees had thorns on them that would go right through my jeans. The thorns on the locust trees were about three inches long! Having been riding on the prairie since we started, I didn't have any chaps. I constantly had to lean left, right or sometimes swing off sideways to keep from getting knocked off by a low hanging branch or having my legs ripped open by the thorns. I was so mad! We were probably close to the wild Kiowas that had started the fire by now. Finally out of the trees, I spurred Paint into a gallop, got the cattle turned and headed back east toward the herd. I kept looking over my shoulder to see if any Indians were fixin' to head me off, but I never saw any. We got back to the herd right when they had started moving north again. No rest for me or those steers. Damn them!

We kept the herd between Salt Creek and Otter Creek. There was a lot of riding from the drag to the flank the rest of the afternoon so we wouldn't lose any of the steers to the creeks. Star was becoming a good cowpony. He developed the knack of hitting a wayward steer with his shoulder or biting him on the top of their tail to get them going the proper way. I thought he was going to be sore the next day as he bumped many a steer who didn't like the idea of crossing the Washita in such a big hurry.

Crossing the Canadian
Tuesday, March 16, 1880

We had camped about eight miles south of the Canadian. Porter's plan for today was to drive the cattle to the river, cross, and bed down on the other side. The plain leading to the river was long and flat. The banks of the river weren't steep at all, but the riverbed was about a half mile or more wide. Porter found a good crossing where the bottom was firm about four miles to the east near Silver City – we didn't want any cattle bogging down in the soft sand.

We passed a 'boot hill' where I saw a grave marker for a William Ward who evidently got himself shot in 1876. There was a herd in front of us that had crossed that morning, and another one coming up behind, so we stopped a mile short of the crossing for the mid-day break and rest. Then we bunched the cattle up and took them across as quickly as we could. I was assigned the upriver side again.

We were crossing from the Chickasaw Indian reservation into the Unassigned Lands, but just to our west a few miles was the Cheyenne-Arapahoe reservation. Yep, the same tribe that was part of Custer's last battle four years ago. And some of these hadn't been on the reservation but a few months. I think they also had a reservation in Montana. I didn't want to get too close! There were no mishaps crossing the river and I didn't get wet at all! I was all ready for Junior and headed him off before he got started. Oh, how I wanted him to be a Cheyenne dinner just to be rid of him! Cookie and Hollis took their wagons to the ferry at Pikey's Crossing about four miles east.

At this point, the Chisholm Trail separated into two different trails. One swung a little to the east a few miles, while the other swung west quite a ways to go by the Darlington Agency near Ft. Reno. The west branch was mainly traveled by freight wagons and stagecoaches. Darlington was the agency for the Cheyenne-Arapaho tribes and also a stage stop for stagecoaches traveling the Chisholm Trail.

We took the east trail but turned the herd back to the west after a mile or so to get out from behind the herd in front of us. We crossed a small creek while keeping parallel to a fair-sized creek to our west. Four miles north of the Canadian, we bedded down the herd for the rest of the day. It had been a fairly warm day and the wind wasn't noticeable.

Back at the chuckwagon, I heard some squawking. It sounded like chickens. Sure enough Cookie had managed to buy a couple of chickens in Silver City. One chicken had already met its doom. I arrived just in time to see Cookie take the other chicken, grab it by it head and swing it around wringing its neck. Mmmmmm. Fried chicken for dinner!

"Cookie can I have the livers? I bet there's catfish in the river."

"Do you have fishing line and hooks?"

"Yes, I like to fish and brought some with me."

"Alright, I'll get the livers for you while you go get your gear."

I dug my army blanket bedroll out of my big canvas bedroll. This smaller bedroll contained the few personal items I owned. I rolled it out a little bit to find the small bag with my few fishing hooks and coiled fishing line in it.

I retrieved the fishing line and a few hooks. "Hollis! Wanta go fishin'?"

"Sure thing, Cory!"

Bird spoke, "I go too."

The three of us went over to the chuckwagon where Cookie gave us the chicken livers from the two unfortunate chickens and some pieces of raw bacon. "Good luck, boys!"

It didn't take us too long to ride back down to the Canadian and we had about three hours before dark. Soon we had three long poles with fishing line tied on the ends, hooks and bait attached. Hollis and I started off with some of the chicken livers and Bird used some of the bacon. Within minutes we started pulling in some big channel cats. I bet they weighed 4-5 pounds. In a couple of hours, we had exhausted our bait and had a dozen nice size fish to show for it. Using our pocket knives, we gutted and cleaned all of the fish right there by the river. We put them in a sack that Cookie had given us and rode back to the camp as heroes. That told us that everyone was tired of beef and beans.

Cookie fried up the catfish in some cornmeal that night. He fried the chickens as well and we had them for breakfast with chicken gravy and biscuits.

These were our best meals on the drive.

The Unassigned Lands
Wednesday, March 17, 1880

I asked Albert why this part of Indian Territory was called the Unassigned Lands and why there were no Indians living here. He said all of Indian Territory, from Arkansas to the Texas Panhandle, and from Kansas to Texas, was given to the Five Civilized Tribes beginning back in the '30's. Since all of the tribes owned slaves, they sided with the South during the War. As a punishment for joining the defeated South, the government took away some of the tribes' lands so now it wasn't assigned to anyone. The ceded lands included the Unassigned Lands here in the central part of the Territory and all lands west of the 98th Meridian. The Cheyennes, Arapahoes, Wichitas, Kiowas, Comanches, and some Apaches were settled west of the 98th Meridian in the '70's.

Far to the north was another piece of land running east and west just south of the Kansas border called the Cherokee Outlet or Cherokee Strip. Originally it belonged to the Cherokee tribe, but since they had sided with the South, they could no longer live on it. They could only use it for hunting. It was called the Outlet since the Cherokees could travel through there on their way to hunt in Colorado. Smaller tribes had since been settled in the east end of the Strip. I think I heard someone say that ranchers were also leasing land from the tribe. Albert said we might have to pay the Cherokees to cross it.

"What's going to happen to this land if no one owns it?"

"Well, Cory, the government owns it, I guess. One of these days, they will probably open it up to settlement by anyone who wants to live in between a bunch of Indian reservations." Albert replied. "There is a bunch of white men who have been trying to get it opened for settlement and there are ranches squatting on the land. We've seen surveyors out and around out here in the middle of nowhere since the early '70's. They must be out there for a reason."

"Cory, did you know that one of Jesse Chisholm's trading posts was on the North Fork of the Canadian about a half dozen miles or so east of here? He died about the time the cattle drives started, but most of the way we go from here was blazed by him. He also had a trading post up on the Arkansas River near Wichita and one down by old Fort Arbuckle. Thus the Chisholm Trail. The early cattle drives came up through that way.

"Is anyone going over to the post? Is there a trading post still there?"

"Probably not. I'm not sure there is anything over there anymore. Fort Reno is about ten miles due west of here and the stagecoaches run near there on the west branch of the Trail. Chisholm is buried about twelve miles west of here. It's probably fairly safe to that point. I think Porter is over there now checking the lay of the land. You, me and the boys will just stay over here in the Unassigned Lands, not worry too much about Injuns, and keep the steers movin' north."

That stupid Junior tried to take off just as we stopped. It took me and Willie both to get him back to the herd. I'm ready to give up a month's wages to be rid of him.

It was getting close to sundown and the wind had stopped blowing. It was quite a bit warmer than the past few days and felt pretty good.

We were dead tired and just about to sit down for supper when we heard someone hail the camp. I had yet to finish unsaddling Nellie. Albert yelled back for them to come on in. I noticed several of our men stepped back out of the campfire light and basically out of sight. In rode some soldiers and about 30 men in civilian clothes. The civilians were all rough looking, but not outlaw rough – poor rough. Their clothes were tattered and had seen better days. They also looked pretty thin. The lieutenant was very polite. I don't recall his name. "Evenin' gents. This here is David Payne and his Boomers. We were wonderin' if you could spare one of your steers? We're on our way to Ft. Reno with these gentlemen and could shore use some fresh meat."

"I hate to see good men go hungry, but these steers all belong to ranchers in Texas," replied Porter.

"We can pay. How much for one?"

"They're bringin' $32 dollars a head in Dodge City right now, so I've heard. But to keep from havin' to drive the critter another month, we can sell it to you for $25."

"25? That's a lot. How 'bout 15?"

"Can't do 15. How about 20?"

"20 it is."

"I'll get one of the boys to go fetch you one."

I jumped to my feet and yelled out, "I'll go!" Before anyone could move, I was on Nellie and riding out to the herd. I had one particular steer in mind and I was so thankful he was easy to find in the bright moonlight.

Some of Payne's men butchered ol' Junior while others started a big fire right outside our camp. I guess I was feeling ornery and decided I would wander over there for a piece of that four-legged no count pack of horns and hide.

There was a soldier standing guard where I approached and I later noticed several posted around their camp. That Payne and his men were prisoners was obvious. "State your business, son," barked the sentry.

"I came to see if I could get a piece of the orneriest steer in the entire herd. I chased that jasper every day and some days twice. I figured on havin' the last laugh."

The guard grinned, "Alright, son. You don't have any weapons on you do you?"

"No, sir."

"Go on ahead."

I walked on into the camp and repeated my request to the lieutenant. "Sure, son. Help yourself. I think there is plenty for everyone and we'll get to Ft. Reno tomorrow, so nothing needs savin'. These men here just haven't had a lot to eat here lately and we just have Army rations."

I had taken my plate with me, and went over to where they were roasting Junior. A man there handed me a stick with a slab of meat on it. It was mostly raw, but I didn't care. It was that no good Junior. I sat down by the fire and just happened to sit next to Capt. Payne. "I don't mean to pry, sir, but may I ask why the Fourth Cavalry is takin' you to Ft. Reno? None of the soldiers are actin' like you are all outlaws, but it's obvious they are takin' you somewhere you don't want to go."

"You're very observant, son. Right where we're sittin' and further to the east, from the Canadian to just north of the Cimarron are Unassigned Lands which were taken away from the Indians back in '66. Two million acres that belongs to the gov'ment that no one can own. I organized the Boomer Colonial Association some years back to try to get the gov'ment to open these lands for settlement. This past February, President Hayes ordered us to quit enterin' these lands. But I won't take no for an answer. Not even from the President himself. There are big ranches using it. These are good lands and there's a lot of poor folks in this country who can use good land.

We made a camp east of here, 20 miles or so, we called it Camp Alice. We were layin' out a town we were goin' to call Ewing, when the Army found us and arrested us. They're takin' us to Ft. Reno and then back up to Kansas. We have 10,000 boomers in the Association, so we'll be back agin and agin until we can get this area opened up for settlement."

"That'll make it hard on the cattle drives if a bunch of settlers put up fences. We won't be able to drive the cattle through," I replied.

"Son, the days of the cattle drives are numbered. It won't be too long before the trains get down to Texas and drivin' cattle to Kansas will be no more."

I didn't have to nighthawk that night and with a full belly, was able to sleep good all night long. I disremember ever having eaten that much.

99

Horse Thieves
Thursday, March 18, 1880

The sunrise was red again this morning and the wind blew hard all morning. By the time we got the herd moving, the Army and the Boomers had moved out.

Charley rode by, "2,406! Yeah boy!" he yelled with a big grin. We had crossed the Red River with 2,401 and yesterday's count was 2,407. Well, I won't be ridin' after Junior today.

We went about six miles and stopped the herd for the midday break.

The afternoon was pure hell. We crossed three sizable creeks, although Albert said the last one was actually a river. The North Fork of the Canadian River. It wasn't any bigger than some of the creeks we had crossed. One creek after another. Chasing steers. Socks was a perfect name for him as in he didn't want to get his socks wet. We would get right down to the water and he acted like he was going to just wade right in. And then at the last second, he would try to jump across! The first time he did it, I wasn't paying attention and almost fell off over backwards. He didn't make it across the North Canadian and as a result – yes, big splash – and I'm all wet again. Stupid pony. I was exhausted. And on top of all that, I'm nighthawking tonight. I ate my beans and beef that night and crawled into bed as fast as I could for a few hours' sleep.

Bird and I were riding nighthawk later that night. I could hear the nighthawks swooping down on the insects they were catching. Hollis was nighthawking the remuda. It was about two hours before dawn. I was over on the east side of the herd riding clockwise. Bird was over on the west side riding counter-clockwise. I saw the almost full moon shining bright and remembered a song that Mama used to sing to us kids,

> *I see the moon,*
> *the moon sees me,*
> *high up in the old oak tree.*
>
> *I see the moon*
> *that shines on me.*
> *Shines on the ones I love.*

I thought I heard something far off to the southeast. It sounded like a bunch of ponies running. I turned south and rode back to the remuda. I saw no sign of Hollis. He should have been around somewhere. The moon was full just a couple of nights ago and still shone very bright - almost like daylight. The horses did seem a little skittish. They were in a large rope corral, but I could tell some were missing. Uh oh, I didn't see Nellie! I was riding Star, there was Paint and Socks, but no Nellie. Something was definitely wrong. Then about that time I heard a moan and saw a saddled pony with no rider. Next to the pony Hollis was laying on the ground. "Hollis! Are you alright? What happened?"

"I think so. Some men jumped me and took some of the ponies."

I helped him back on his pony and made sure he was steady enough not to fall off.

I took off back to the herd in time to see Bird coming around, "Bird! Some men have stolen some of our ponies." Go get help. I'll go see if I can keep them in sight." Bird nodded and took off. I took off in the direction of the sound I heard earlier.

I rode southeast and could see fairly well in the moonlight, but really couldn't see tracks on the ground. Then I smelled dust in the air and was also getting close to the North Fork of the Canadian. This must be their trail. I turned east and from time to time could see where the ground had been churned up by running hooves. I spurred Star and we took off after them. But I went too fast.

I topped a hill and rode right in amongst them. They had slowed to a walk, thinking they weren't being followed. Not being able to see over the hill, I had ridden right down on top of them. There were three of them. The closest one to me stopped, turned his pony and pulled out his gun.

"Well, well, what do we have here?" said Snaggle Tooth. This fellow looked like he had been rode hard and put away wet one too many times.

I replied, "We had some ponies get loose and I came to take them back to the herd. I'm with a cattle drive heading to Kansas. I appreciate you boys catchin' them for me."

I heard laughing behind me. "Son, you don't seem to understand the situation, we found these hosses just wanderin' around. Theys are our hosses now." Tuck, keep 'em movin'. We'll be along." The third man turned his pony and drove Nellie and the other ponies away to the east.

"Check their left shoulders," I tried to say calmly, although my heart was beating so hard I thought it was about to bust, "the Rocking P is our herd brand. Those are our ponies."

"And you figure to take them back all by yourself, huh? Well, I will say you do have spunk." He was carrying a rifle and he waved it at me menacingly. "Get off your hoss."

I was in a fix. I climbed down. Rifle man said, "Take that pistol of yours with two fingers of your left hand and throw it over there. Joe, cover him." Joe must be Snaggle Tooth's name. Joe, held his pistol on me, while Rifle man came over and went through my pockets. I had $3.57 in one vest pocket and a handful of .45 shells in the other. He put my money in his pocket and started to feed my bullets into his rifle. "Boy, I'm lucky you came along, I was down to three shells. Now I can take on a whole bunch of cowboys." He grinned menacingly.

My only thought now, well two thoughts as not getting shot was thought number one, was to stall them until the men from the herd caught up to us. If they could find us in the dark that is. But if there was any shooting, some of my friends could get shot and possibly killed. About that time I thought I heard something back to the west, "Mister, that's the only money I have. And the only bullets and you've got my favorite pony. Where're you taking them?"

"There's always a market for good hosses, young man. And you won't be needing your money, bullets or that hoss of yours."

Then we all heard my cowboys coming. I had a flashback to Dave, telling me to be careful and not mix up my .45 shells with the .44-40 shells as they wouldn't fit in the rifle's chamber. In the dark, Rifle man hadn't noticed that I was carrying the 1858 Remingtons with the conversion cylinders, but had assumed I was carrying a .44-40 pistol like most cowboys did since all of the rifles were .44-40s. I knew then that when he levered a .45 cartridge into his rifle that it would jam. I was also going to bet that Snaggle

Tooth wouldn't shoot toward Rifle man. They both heard the boys coming and turned toward the sound at the same time. Rifle man pushed the lever on his rifle forward and the split second it started back the gun jammed and it startled him. As he looked down at his jammed rifle, I lunged at him and grabbed his rifle with both hands. Twisting it toward him, I kneed him in the groin at the same time. He bent forward and let go of the rifle. I swung the butt of the rifle and it hit him right under his chin. He fell over backwards and dropped like a rock. I swung the rifle on Snaggle Tooth hoping he couldn't see well enough in the dawn to see the lever wasn't closed. "Drop it or I'll blow your brains out!" And to my surprise – he did! I kept the rifle on him, walked over, picked up my pistol, wiped it against my jeans and pointed it at him.

Just then the boys rode over the hill with Bird, Porter and Albert in the lead. Bird had been able to follow our trail in the moonlight on a dead run.

"Cory! What do you have here?" Porter shouted as they rode up.

"These fellers stole our ponies, sir. There's one more of them trailin' the ponies just up ahead. These two were stealin' Nellie and now were robbin' me. I think they were fixin' to kill me. I took exception to it."

Rifle man was just starting to stir. Albert and Bird grabbed him and tied his hands behind his back. Porter had his gun on Snaggle Tooth. "Tie this one up too, boys." It seemed like just a few minutes later that the rest of the men returned with the rest of the ponies.

"That other fellow took one look at us and took off like he was shot out of a cannon. Shall we go catch him, boss?"

"No," Porter replied, "We'll take care of these two and get back to the herd. Cookie and Harley are the only ones there and Hollis may be hurt."

"Whatcha gonna do with us," Snaggle Tooth whined.

"We're goin' to have a necktie party in your honor," Porter said and he wasn't smiling.

I wasn't sure what a necktie party was at the time, but those two were the first men I had ever seen hung.

I'd best not describe it here.

Friday, March 19, 1880

We crossed a road heading off to the southeast. Albert said this was Jesse Chisholm's Wagon Road. The first cattle drives to Abilene came up from down that way. Passing by where Fort Arbuckle used to be on Wildhorse Creek, on the north side of the Arbuckle Mountains, and turning north here. The trail we had been traveling for the last couple of weeks was originally called The Abilene Trail. Now everybody calls it Chisholm's Trail.

We drove the herd straight north. At the noon break we stopped about two miles north of a small creek. The area was real flat with a hill less than a mile off to the west. I rode over to the top of that hill and could see probably 20 miles to the eastern horizon. The land around was all prairie with no trees and good grass as far as you could see in any direction. There were a half a dozen herds in sight from the hill to the east and to the west.

Easter was on March 28th this year. This would be a great spot to watch the sun come up way over on the horizon.

We flushed several covey of quail during the afternoon. Even though the grass wasn't very tall, I'd rarely see them before they would thunder up right under the pony's nose. Every time, Paint would buck a little like it scared him. I'd bet good cash money that stupid pony knew those quail were there before they flew up. He just wanted an excuse to try and throw me. It's amazing how much noise eight to ten little birds could make when taking flight. The cattle acted like they didn't even notice them. I think a lot of the steers can walk in their sleep.

That evening at supper, Albert told us that some herds turned off the Chisholm Trail and headed northwest after crossing the North Fork of the Canadian. This trail variation was known as Fletcher's Crossing. Not sure who Fletcher was. He must not have been very afraid of wild Indians. Those herds traveled close to the North Fork until they were south of Dodge City. We won't go that way because it would take us right across the Cheyenne-Arapaho reservation even though we weren't that far from the Strip. We didn't have enough men to protect the herd if we got into a fight. We'll just go around.

I had nighthawk tonight from midnight to two a.m. The three-quarters moon set before I got out there. Nellie and I started off riding clock-wise. It was nice and dark, but it was a clear night and I could see fairly well by the star light. Well except for maybe close to the ground. There were millions of stars and the Milky Way covered a good portion of the night sky. I was hoping to see some shooting stars tonight.

Whenever I turned to the north, I looked for the Big Dipper and the North Star. I know the older guys can tell time by the stars. I need to ask Albert or Charley. I bet they know how.

Saturday, March 20, 1880

As we rode north and northwest to join back up with the west branch of the Trail, we came upon a large creek off to the west that was running south to north. This was Uncle John's Creek. We began to follow parallel to it as Albert said it flowed into Kingfisher Creek. We would cross the Cimarron near where Kingfisher Creek flowed into it.

As I topped a rise near the creek, I heard a great commotion. It sounded like someone was getting murdered. There was a loud ear-piercing screeching and then lots of squabbling. Looking to see that the steers were walking along just fine, I turned Paint over that way to investigate. Sitting high up in a tree was one of those red-tail hawks. Diving at the hawk was a bunch of crows. Whenever a crow got too close, the hawk would fly up in the air, turn upside down and try to rake the crow with its talons.

I hated crows. We had some pecan trees on our place back home and Papa would make us kids go down there in the Fall and throw rocks at the crows to keep them from eating our pecans. As soon as we'd leave they'd fly right back. There was no end to it. I wanted to shoot them all, but we couldn't afford the shotgun shells. Stupid crows.

The crows were so busy fighting with the hawk, that they hadn't noticed me riding up. I pulled my pistol out, took a steady aim with both hands, and shot at a crow that was sitting in a nearby tree. Big mistake.

Looking back, I guess I should have warned ol' Paint what I was fixin' to do. That pistol went off pretty close to his ear. Needless to say it was a big surprise to him! He jumped sideways as he threw his head down and his hind legs straight up in the air. With me holding the reins with my left hand and the pistol with both hands, I had no chance. I went flying and Paint took off in a dead run. I swear I could hear those crows laughing as they flew away.

I got up off the ground and dusted myself off. It took me a while to find my pistol. I had walked about a mile before Charley saw me and came riding up, "What's wrong, Cory? Where's your pony?"

All I could reply was "stupid crows."

Spring Arrives
Sunday, March 21, 1880

It was the first day of Spring – equal parts night and day. I like it when the days get longer. I seem to have more energy. When the days start getting shorter in the Fall, my energy level seems to drop. When the day starts at 7:30 and it's dark by 5:30, yuck! I'd rather it be light at 4:30 a.m. and not get dark until after 8:00 p.m.

It was a perfect first day of Spring – all warm and sunny. This was the first day in a long time I could ride with just my shirt and vest on. No coat, no slicker, no wind. Even Nellie seemed more perky today than usual.

As I was riding my two hour shift around the herd this Sunday afternoon, Albert rode up beside me, "Cory did you know that Easter always falls on the first Sunday after the first full moon that rises after the March Equinox? The moon will be full this week, so next Sunday is Easter!"

"Wow, I didn't know that. I've always wondered why Easter is on a different day every year. Sometimes in March. Sometimes in April."

"Now you know. Did you know the word Equinox is derived from Latin, meaning "equal night?"

"Albert, what's the difference between an equinox and a solstice? Are they the same thing?

"Not really, Cory. The Equinoxes – equal night and equal day – are used for the first day of Spring and the first day of Fall. The solstices are the terms for the longest day of the year – the first day of Summer, and the shortest day of the year – the first day of Winter."

"Equinox – Equal. That shouldn't be too hard for me to remember."

"Also, did you know there are man-made rock formations in the Rocky Mountains that line up with the equinoxes? These are called medicine wheels. I've seen one up in the Big Horns that is on top of a mountain. A Crow Indian told me that no one knows who built it or when. It was already there when the Crow people came into that country. The Crow said he knew of other medicine wheels in the mountains."

"How did these ancient people know when was the first day of Spring, Summer, Fall and Winter, so they could line up all these rocks?"

"That, young Cory, I don't know."

Crossing the Cimarron
Monday, March 22, 1880

We kept Uncle John's Creek to our west and drove the cattle at a good pace. Porter wanted to cross the Cimarron today. There were big storm clouds to the west which meant the river could get up fast and strand us on this side for a couple of days or more. After 9 or 10 hard miles, we got to Kingfisher Creek. It wasn't much smaller than the North Fork of the Canadian, but had steeper banks. Porter decided to stay east of Kingfisher Creek and cross Trail Creek instead. It was well after 2 o'clock before we got the herd across. We stopped the herd within sight of the Cimarron for a short break.

Over to the east we could see Red Fork Ranch also known as Red Fork Station and its stockade style buildings. The name Station was due to it being a stop for the semi-weekly stagecoaches going from Arkansas City, Kansas to Ft. Sill.

Albert said the Cimarron used to be called the Red Fork of the Arkansas, thus the name Red Fork Ranch. This was a trading post on the north side of the river. They actually have pens where cattle could be kept and the cowboys could take time off to rest and relax without having to watch over their herds. Some herds were driven up in the late fall and wintered here on the range surrounding the ranch. Although I couldn't tell for sure, there seemed to be a lot of cattle over that way.

Starting around 4 o'clock, we pushed the steers into the river just east of Kingfisher Creek. The Cimarron was much like the Canadian – the riverbed was wide and the water was just deep enough that the longhorns had to swim. I could tell the river flooded drastically from time to time by the amount of brush high up in some of the trees along the riverbank.

As Homer and the leaders reached the middle of the river, the steers on the upstream side apparently decided they weren't going to make it across and tried to turn around. They swam downstream and then angled back toward the south shore. They then ran into the steers swimming across and were turned back north. Soon a hundred or so of the first steers into the river were swimming in a circle. None were trying to get to the other side. As more and more steers tried to cross the circle grew larger and more chaotic.

"They're going to drown if we can't get them to the other side!" yelled Albert.

All of a sudden, Bird plunged his horse into the river right into the middle of the milling cattle. By that time, Homer was approaching the far side for about the sixth time and was looking very weary. Bird guided his pony right up to Homer and leaped upon his back! Pulling his pistol, Bird held the pistol right by Homer's right ear and shot into the water. Once! Twice! Homer plunged to his left almost going under the water. He struggled to stay upright with Bird clinging to his back. Homer finally straighten up and turned for the north shore with the rest of the herd following behind him.

As they climbed up the bank, Bird rolled off backwards and sprinted to the nearest cottonwood, where he kept the big tree between himself and the half wild longhorns crossing the river. Thanks to Bird's heroics, I don't think we lost a single steer.

There was lots of fine, soft sand on the north side of the river. The cattle's hooves plunged down knee deep. Some of the steers did sink in some soft spots and we had to rope them by their horns and pull them out. I could tell which ones had been caught in the milling as there were over a hundred that plopped to the ground as soon as they found solid footing. They were all tuckered out.

I was getting better at roping and Star was a good cow pony. It was after dark before we had all of the cattle and all of the ponies over to the north side. We moved the herd a couple miles north to get away from the sand hills along the river, and then west a couple more miles to get away from the herds at the Red Fork Ranch.

We were still in the Unassigned Lands, and turning to the northwest we would still be in the Unassigned Lands. The north boundary of the Cheyenne-Arapaho reservation stopped at the Cimarron.

The Cheyenne participated with the Sioux at the battle where Custer was killed just four years ago. Papa had read in the Spanish Fort paper recently that one of the Sioux medicine men, Sitting Bull, and some of his people were still on the loose and heading for Canada. I was still real nervous about being so close to them.

I found out later, that the Cheyenne in the Custer fight were Northern Cheyenne and on a reservation in Montana. The Indians here in Indian Territory were Southern Cheyenne and had been working for peace for some years.

Matthew Wolfe
Wednesday, March 24, 1880

Matthew Wolfe was our pony wrangler. He took care of anything that had to do with the ponies and herded the remuda during the day. He had the forearms of a blacksmith. Originally, I had assumed I would rope my mount whenever I needed one, like Paint on that first day. However, to keep the half-wild ponies relatively calm, all mounts were lassoed by Matthew since they all got to know him very well. Matthew knew each and every pony and whose string it belonged to. I started the drive by telling him which pony I wanted and after a few days, he would know which pony of mine came up in the rotation and have him roped and ready for me in the mornings, at mid-day, or for nighthawking.

At the end of the day, he and Hollis would drive stakes into the ground, and loop a single rope through them to form a loose corral. The horses had been trained sufficiently after a few weeks on the trail to stay within this enclosure. The ponies also got to graze along the Trail as they slowly followed the steers.

The remuda stayed some distance behind the herd. The ponies learned quickly not to get too close to the longhorns if they didn't have to. They could end up getting scratched or even gored by those long sharp horns. There were about 50 ponies in our remuda. I had the use of four. Porter and Albert had six each. Porter had the six best ponies. Of course, he would ride miles and miles every day. Usually on the same pony. Albert had the next six best ponies. I thought all of my ponies were pretty good. I had inherited Sandy's ponies, so he must have been fairly early in the selection process. Anyhow, Porter had acquired some really good stock for the drive.

I think ponies eat a lot more than cows do although it seems like either one will eat all the time if you let them. It seems like the grass goes right through them. Cattle with their three stomachs will kinda spit up the grass they've eaten and chew on it some more when they are laying down. Since ponies walk faster than the cattle do, they can spend more time eating during the day and still keep up with the cattle.

Not to get off the subject of Matthew and the remuda, but I also noticed that all of the cattle seem to walk everyday in the same position within the herd. Homer was always up front. He rarely let any steer get ahead of him. But the steers beside or near him were always the same ones. Same with the laggards or slowpokes. They were always the same lazy ones.

Right before the midday break, I noticed that Socks was favoring his left front leg. I took him over to Matthew for him to check. Matthew bent over, leaned against Socks' shoulder, pulled up Sock's leg and put it between his legs. "Thar's your problem, Cory boy. Your pony has thrown a shoe. It's like he's runnin' around barefoot. I'll have him fixed up good as new in no time."

Matthew went to the supply wagon where he had several boxes of horseshoes. "Different sizes, 'cause ponies have different size feet just like we do." I have no forge out here on the prairie, so we have to make do with these. He pulled out a horseshoe, picked up Sock's leg again, held it between his knees and held the shoe to the hoof. "Perfect!" he said.

Matthew got his wooden tool box from the supply wagon and set it on the ground by Socks. The toolbox was about a foot and a half long with sides six inches tall. The ends were about ten inches tall and pointed at the top.

Connecting the top of the ends was a thick round wooden rod for a handle.

Getting his nippers, Matthew picked up Sock's leg and put it between his knees. He carefully trimmed the hoof wall just a little and then cleaned out some dirt and a small stone that were embedded in his hoof.

Next, he hammered the shoe into Sock's outer hoof using small nails and a small hammer. It looked like the ends of the nails came out on the side of the hoof. Matthew cut off the sharp ends of the nails and then used a clincher to bend the rest of the nail so it was almost flush with the hoof wall. He then got a rasp to smooth the edge of the hoof where it met the shoe.

"Good as new, Cory boy!" Matthew then examined Sock's other three hoofs by picking them up one at a time and placing them between his legs. "These all look fine."

"Matthew, how do you shoe a pony that isn't broke or is half broke like most of our ponies? I'm surprised that Socks stood this still for you."

"Socks is it? That's a good name. Sometimes, Cory boy, we have to snub the pony down so he can't move his head, then rope the leg we want to work on. Then we hoist it up so he can't really move without fallin' down. Once a pony has been shod, they are smart enough to realize these iron shoes are better for their feet than being unshod. It's like you wearin' boots instead of going barefoot. Horses in general are pretty smart and catch on fast."

"Thanks, Matthew. Where'd you learn to do all this?"

"My dad was a blacksmith back in Arkansas. As soon as I was big enough to pump the bellows, I helped him at his smithy."

"How did you end up out here on a cattle drive?"

"Being a blacksmith is hot, hard work. Pumpin' those bellows constantly to get or keep the fire hot enough, poundin' on metal all day shapin' horseshoes, hinges, mountin' the iron wagon tires on wheels, all bent over all day. My pa would get to where he could barely stand up straight after a long day's work. I decided that wasn't for me. And I wanted to see the west. I didn't know anythin' about cattle, but I knew horses and blacksmithin', so here I am. This is my third drive."

"Thanks, Matthew."

"Sure thing. I'll check your other ponies over the next day or two. We don't want to have them throw shoes or go lame on you."

The Storm
Friday, March 26, 1880

I had heard of tornados or twisters or cyclones but I had never seen one. When I woke up this morning, there was an ominous feeling in the air. I couldn't quite put my hand on it. Unlike other mornings, I didn't hear the call of the meadowlark or the quail. It was going to be another windy day, but it was considerably warmer than in days past. The air even felt thicker. I tied my slicker onto the back of my saddle in case it rained, and Paint and I rode out to the left flank again.

I could tell the cattle were restless and seemed mighty jumpy. There were lots of low white clouds in the sky, none of which seemed very threatening. We continued northwest staying a couple miles north the Cimarron. Albert said this part of the trail was called the Cimarron Cutoff and we were leaving the Chisholm Trail behind. The Cimarron will take us into Kansas and just to the south of Dodge City. We were still in the Unassigned Lands.

We made about 7-8 miles before the midday rest. The ground was very flat and the going easy. We stayed north of the river as there were sand hills right along and just to the north of it. For lunch, Cookie made us roast beef sandwiches. He could drive the wagon faster than the cattle would walk, so a lot of days he went on ahead and made camp well before we got there. I guess that's when he had time to bake bread. He must have made this bread the night before.

Albert was talking, "About six years ago, they found the charred body of a teamster named Pat Hennessey tied to the wagon wheel of his burned out wagon. His fellow teamsters lay dead and scalped nearby. All killed by Injuns. That was about 3-4 miles northeast of here."

Six years ago! That wasn't that long ago. Some of the Indians had been put on the reservation before then. Were these reservation Indians that did that? Or some renegades? I'm sleeping with one eye open tonight! (I never could do that although I tried many a night). We started the herd back on the trail close to 2 o'clock. The sky to the west was dark and the wind had shifted from the south to the southwest. The little white clouds were gone and in the distance I could see several clouds growing taller by the minute. The cattle remained very skittish but stayed in a steady walk, and as usual, always trying to stop and eat the green grass along the way.

About 4 or 5 o'clock, I felt cool air and looked to the west to see that all those tall clouds had joined together to form one huge cloud. The top of that cloud extended halfway across the sky. It must have had a lot of rain in it because the sunlight wasn't coming through the middle of it. The cloud was almost black. The bottom of the cloud had to be more than a mile across and the whole thing was spinning clockwise. And, the bottom of this huge cloud was getting lower and lower to the ground. Albert came riding back toward me, "We're going to circle up the herd for the night and hope that storm goes north of us. Round 'em!"

All of us starting moving the herd in a clockwise direction to turn the leaders back into the herd. By now the cattle knew this meant it was time to quit for the day but they were very vocal and uneasy. I knew the storm was upsetting them if not scaring them. I rode back into camp where Porter was calling a meeting. "Men, we're all going to have to circle the herd continuously until the storm has passed. We can't risk a stampede. Get a fresh mount. Half of you ride clockwise, the others counter-clockwise. We'll take turns peelin' off to grab a bite to eat. Cookie, keep the coffee on and we'll all need some more to eat later this evenin' and maybe into the night. Any questions?"

"Yeah," asked one of the hands, "why is Hollis hidin' under his wagon."

"Don't you worry about Hollis. You just worry about cattle."

"Yes sir!"

I changed my saddle to Socks and walked over to Hollis. He was literally shaking underneath that wagon. "Hollis, buddy, are you alright?"

"N-n-n-no. I been scared to death of storms ever since I got caught out in one and got hit in the head with a hail ball."

"What's a hail ball?"

"These storms can have hail bigger than your fist. I got hit in the head and my back when I was little. It knocked me out and I had a big bruise on my back for weeks. Momma said it could have killed me."

That explained a few things about Hollis and maybe why he was mentally slow. I had never seen any hail bigger than pea size. Anyhow, he was going to stay underneath that wagon until the hail threat had passed. That was for sure.

I joined the other riders and we rode around and around that herd until after midnight. It rained hard but the major portion of the storm did pass to the north of us. I had never seen so much lightning or heard so much thunder. Lightning would flash and in about two seconds a loud clap of thunder would follow. It was actually a pretty awesome sight.

Just before sundown, Albert had pointed to near the top of the cloud where it was a greenish color. "If there is green in the cloud, there's hail. Hollis is smart to stay under the wagon. We're the dumb ones."

We were able to keep the herd settled down and passed the rest of the night without incident. I got about four hours of sleep and then the sun was up and time to hit the trail again.

Bullfoot Station
Saturday, March 27, 1880

Once we crossed the Cimarron, the land stayed pretty flat about a mile north of the river and further. It was easy walking for cattle and for ponies, and the men riding those ponies. My back spasms were pretty much gone although I could feel my back tighten up some if I twisted it unexpectantly.

The Cimarron River flowed from northwest to southeast here, so now we were angling northwest toward Dodge City. The Cutoff followed the Cimarron northwest close to a point just south of Dodge City. If we had kept going straight north on the Chisholm Trail, we would have gone near Caldwell, Wichita, Newton and Abilene, or even a little further west to Ellsworth. We had heard that the railroad was extending on south to Caldwell and that Kansas was going to let the herds come there. Not sure when that was going to happen.

Since the land was pretty flat, I missed riding to the top of the tall hills. It was one of my favorite things to do so I could see for miles and miles. The downside was that the taller the hill, the more likely a deep creek or river crossing was waiting at the bottom. Taking a herd of 2,400 steers across a deep creek or across a river were two different things. The river crossings had shallower banks and a flat approach usually of a mile or more. A number of cattle could all cross at the same time because they all spread out to drink. If there was a steer blocking the trail, the other steers would go one way or the other and could spread out along the bank. The narrower the trails down to the river the longer it took for them to drink and get across. Once we got them started, getting across didn't take so long. Of course, the water was sometimes deeper and sometimes there was a current you and your pony had to swim across, plus occasional soft sand where cattle could bog down and had to be pulled out. No doubt about it, crossing any river could be an adventure unto itself. But they usually didn't slow us down as much as a big creek could.

Now crossing some of those creeks we encountered – that's another story. Some of these creeks were 15 – 20 feet deep, 30 yards across, and had high and steep banks. We had to find trails down to the bottom and up the other side to get the cattle across. Sometimes there were only 2-3 trails and the cattle had to cross single file. Yeah, crossing a deep creek could take us almost half a day and there was always a stupid few steers that would spook and literally go right over the steep bank, sometimes rolling down to the bottom. Luckily we never had one break a leg or get seriously hurt.

Porter sent Hollis and me over to Bullfoot Station which was a half dozen miles east of us to replenish some of our supplies. Again, the men gave us some money and we made a list of the tobacco, cigarette papers, matches, candy and supplies that each man wanted. The ground was considerably flatter and seemed smoother than the ride to Duncan's Station so many days ago. We kept a sharp lookout for Indians as we were told we were near the area where Pat Hennessey had been tortured and murdered. We never saw any though.

The prairie was flat as far as the eye could see. About a mile out, I noticed the ground looked rather bare. I leaned over for a closer look. The ground was bare with hardly any grass, but the track went southwest to northeast. The cattle herds go southeast to northwest. I couldn't figure it out. Why would anyone drive a large amount of cattle in this direction? Except the ground wasn't really churned up. There were no hoof prints. We rode on another mile or so until we came to a little creek that had a few trees along it. They were pretty scraggly. It looked like the top half of the trees had been twisted off. That's it! Last night's storm must have had a twister that was so strong, it pulled the grass out of the ground. It must not have been touching the ground when it hit these trees or didn't dip down into the creek low enough to pull them out of the ground.

Wow! Glad that twister didn't go over us. It would have scattered us to kingdom come!

We had gone about four miles when I saw something sticking up out of the short grass. "Hollis, let's go see what that is." Hollis swung the wagon more toward the east. Getting closer, we jumped off the wagon to find a cross made of sticks and bound together with rawhide. It had been knocked over so that one arm was in the dirt and the other arm was sticking straight up into the sky. There was a bare spot about the size of a man's grave. Maybe this was where they buried Pat Hennessey four years ago, but I didn't see anything that looked like the graves of the other teamsters. It looked like a cattle herd or two had been driven right over the site. Realizing what this might be gave me the chills right down my spine. Made a body take a good slow look around although there weren't supposed to be any Indians in this part of the country anymore. I had nightmares several nights after that just imagining Hennessey being scalped, tied to his wagon wheel, and being burned alive.

Bullfoot Station had seen better days. There was a good water well here. But the big cattle drives hadn't been this way in four years, and the stagecoaches usually rolled by without stopping. The Southwestern Stage Coach Company had its headquarters in Caldwell. The stage's first day stopped at Skeleton Ranch where there was a big spring. The second day the stage went on to the Savannah Stage Station down on Kingfisher Creek. The teams were changed about halfway at Buffalo Springs, which was about five miles north of here. So no stopping at Bullfoot Station.

Bullfoot Station got its name from a big indentation in the ground which looked, well, like a big bull's hoof print. The station itself was pretty much a soddie. It had big bricklike chunks of prairie grass sod almost a foot thick laid alternatingly like bricks. The inside of the station had some cedar posts for supporting the ceiling planks and there were large sheets of canvas laid out on top of the cedar planks to keep the dirt and bugs from raining down on the occupants. The counter was made of planks as well with goods on rough shelves behind. We were able to fill most of our order for the men and headed back west to the herd.

I saw several shooting stars that night. The night was so clear and the air smelled so fresh after the storms. I made a wish on each one. First one was for me to make it to Kansas safely. Next a wish for blessings for Mama and Papa. Then blessings for Johnnie and Ida. The last shooting star I saw I thought of little Lizzie and her last words.

Easter
Sunday, March 28, 1880

Mama and Papa always made us kids get up in the dark (it always seemed like the middle of the night), to go watch the sunrise on Easter morning. Mama said that was what all good Christians do to celebrate Jesus coming back from the dead, rolling that big stone away and going up to heaven to be with God. I never did mind because watching the sunrise is one of my favorite things to do.

Being out here on the prairie, I have seen many sunrises. The best spot is high on a hill where I can see the horizon miles and miles away. Over here north of the Cimarron, there are no hills. There are no trees. I can see the horizon but it is only seems a few miles away. It was a good sunrise anyway as there were no trees to block it.

"Cory, do you believe in God?" Hollis asked me later that day.

"Yeah. I guess I always have. Mama and Papa always made us go to church to learn about God, Jesus and the Holy Ghost."

"What's the Holy Ghost?"

"The preacher said it was like holy spirits that kinda watch over you. Mama said it was like havin' guardian angels watch over you. Maybe that's what they call God's angels. I remember when I was little, we had just moved to Texas. I was hikin' along the bottom of a creek down by the house when I saw this little cave in the side of the creek bank just under a bunch of tree roots. The creek had washed out the dirt from around half of the tree's roots and it looked like there was a little cave up under there. It wasn't that big of a cave but I was small enough that I could climb up in there. I was down in the creek, which was dry, and the hole was just up in the bank higher than my head. I started to climb up the bank to crawl into the hole, when I had this strange feeling that I shouldn't do it. Then I had another strange feeling that I should. Then I shouldn't. It was like there was an argument in my mind going on – back and forth. I just stood there for a little while unable to make up my mind. Then I looked up and saw a rattlesnake comin' out of that hole. Oh, was I glad I hadn't climbed up in there. I went home and told Papa about the hole with the rattlesnake and since it was so close to the house, he wanted me to show it to him."

"The next day, I took Papa and my Uncle Dave down to the creek to show them the little cave where I had seen the snake come out. They both had shovels with them. They started diggin' into the creek bank and found it was a whole entire nest of rattlesnakes. I think they killed 27 all together."

"And to think you almost crawled into that hole."

"Yep. Mama said that strange feelin' I had tellin' me not to climb in there was my guardian angels lookin' after me."

"But do you believe in God?"

"Sure, Hollis. I just know he's all around us. How can you not look up into the sky and see the millions of stars and not wonder how they got there? How can you see a baby calf born, or baby kitten born and not wonder who made them?

I just never really feel alone, even when I'm all by myself. I guess the Holy Ghost is always with me too. Yeah, Hollis, there's no doubt in my mind there's God, Jesus and the

guardian angels that look after me. I think the preacher calls them all the Trinity.
I think I actually feel closer to God out here in nature than I do in church.

Yeah, Hollis, no doubt at all."

Tuesday, March 30, 1880

As I've said before, there just weren't that many trees. There were usually some willows and cottonwoods along the rivers and sometimes the creeks. But with the cattle herds going this way for some years now, a lot of those had been cut for firewood. Poking around camp that day, I noticed the canvas sheet hanging under the chuckwagon didn't have any firewood. "Cookie, what are we going to do for firewood?"

"We'll be pickin' up cow chips, Cory. When there is no wood to burn, we pick up cow chips as we go along and toss them there under the wagons. Just like the pioneers did on the Oregon trail with buffalo chips. They make a pretty hot fire. It just takes a lot of them. And, of course, you hope the ones you pick up, aren't fresh," he said with a wink and a smile.

The moon was almost half full that night and as I rode around the herd I wondered how people like Albert and Charley could tell time without the moon. I knew the sun went down around seven o'clock this time of year and rose around seven o'clock the next morning. If there was a moon in the sky, you could take note of its position at sundown. So, if it was straight up at seven o'clock, you knew it would set around one o'clock in the morning. I could also tell time by knowing that it took about 30 minutes to ride slowly around the herd. There was always another nighthawk riding in the opposite direction, so we'd meet up every 15 minutes. If I counted the times we'd pass, I would know when my two or four hours was up.

Charley Opperude was riding with me tonight and the moon had just set. When we passed, I asked him, "Charley, how do you tell time after the moon goes down?"

"Cory, look to the north. See the Big Dipper there? A bunch of bright stars that look like pot with a handle. Now those two stars at the end point to a rather faint star. See it? That is the North Star also known as Polaris. Those two stars in the Big Dipper pointing at it are called the pointer stars. The North Star is the only star in the sky that doesn't move. Since the Earth revolves, all of the stars seem to revolve with it. Only the North Star stays in the same spot. Anywhere you are, if you can see the Big Dipper and find the North Star, you always will know which direction is north."

"You can also use the North Star to tell time at night. Draw a line from the North Star going straight up. Now when those two pointer stars are pointing straight down at the North Star along that line it is midnight. Now imagine you are looking at a giant clock with the North Star in the middle. The entire clock is 24 hours. The two pointer stars will tell you what time it is with the catch that they go counter-clockwise. So when they point to the left of midnight, that will be one o'clock, then keep going left to two o'clock. If they are pointing to the right of midnight, then it will be ten o'clock. Straight down will be noon, which of course you won't be able to see it then. Follow?"

"Yes, I think so."

"As the months go by, the Earth changes position, so your star clock also changes. A couple of months from now, midnight will be where 4 o'clock is now. Since we are close to the Spring Equinox, straight up will be midnight. Close to the time of the Autumn Equinox, midnight will be straight down. It isn't exact but it can get you pretty close. If you are outside all of the time throughout the year, it's easy to keep track of."

"What if it's cloudy and there's no stars?"

"Then you're on your own, son. But out here you'll get a feel for the time and never have to look at a watch. Unless you fall asleep and lose track, that is."

One thing about being out on the trail is, you lose track of days. If we didn't stop every Sunday to rest, I don't know that I would ever know which day of the week it was. When it was time for me to turn in, I noticed Albert riding out to ride nighthawk. "Hey Albert, I didn't know you ever nighthawked."

"Well, young Cory. Just between you and me, I wanted an excuse to be up tonight. Tomorrow's April Fool's Day."

I could tell he was grinning real big although there was no moon tonight.

April Fools
Thursday, April 1, 1880

This morning started out as usual with everyone getting up before sunrise. Except Willie couldn't find his boots.

After breakfast and finally finding his boots up top of the chuckwagon, Willie was a little bit miffed. Someone had already saddled his pony for him, so he climbed on, sat down, and that pony started bucking like nobody's business! I'd never seen that pony buck like that. It was like he had gone crazy. In no time, Willie went sailing through the air landing in a heap on the ground. He was up in a flash and madder than all get out. His pony was still bucking. Willie caught him, calmed him down and jumped back in the saddle. That pony went mad. It was jumping and bucking and turning in a circle so fast it was all a blur, and in no time Willie came flying out to crash on the ground.

This time the pony took off and one of the other men had to chase it and rope it. Bringing the pony back to the camp, Willie muttered something about not riding that pony again. Taking off the saddle, he threw it on the ground. He grabbed the saddle blanket and threw it on top of the saddle where it landed upside down. There on the saddle blanket was a handful of cockleburs. Everybody saw the cockleburs about the same time as I did and the whooping and hollering began. There were men rolling on the ground holding their stomachs. I only thought Willie had been mad. He was so mad now, I thought he might shoot us all. Since he sometimes picked on Hollis and me, I thought it best not to laugh where he could see me. I could save it up for later.

I saddled up Socks and looking over my saddle saw Albert looking away and grinning from ear to ear.

When we stopped that night and gathered around the chuckwagon, I could tell that Willie was still pretty mad. I had got in before him and was sitting eating my beans and bacon when he came and stood right over me so close I couldn't eat anymore. "Did you put those cockleburs under my saddle this mornin'?

"Nope."

"You're a liar."

I could tell he was mad and was wanting to get even with someone. With me being the youngest and smallest, I guess that someone was me. I consider myself easygoing but won't take any crap from anybody. "I don't lie. It'd be best if you didn't call me a liar."

He knocked my plate out of my hands and I tackled him around the knees. I knew I couldn't wrestle with him as he was four years older than me, and bigger and stronger. I rolled free in a crouch and as he came up off the ground, I sprang up while swinging my right hand and hit him on his chin as hard as I could. Although I hadn't really fought much as a boy, mostly just wrestling, I remember Dave telling me once to aim my punch a few inches beyond where I was going to connect so there would be more power in the punch.

My punch caught Willie right under the chin and with me straightening my legs and almost jumping up at the same time, my punch had enough power to knock him over and onto his back. He rolled over and got up slowly rubbing his chin. "Well, I guess it wasn't you." He turned and walked away.

That punch felt mighty good and I felt relieved about not getting beat up. The knuckles on my hand hurt for two days.

But it was a good hurt.

Friday, April 2, 1880

We kept the herd moving northwest still staying about two miles north of the river. Out here the terrain was flat and easy going. Because of the flatness, the cattle bunched up more than traveling in a long line, so it was easier to keep them moving without having to ride up and back all the time.

In the afternoon, I counted 18 buzzards circling in the sky to the south and not too far away. The cattle were moving in good order, so I thought I would take a quick ride to see what the buzzards were having for dinner. We rode across a little sand hill near the river and saw two coyotes eating on a dead deer. The deer had an arrow sticking out of its side. Evidently the arrow hadn't killed the deer outright and it got away from whoever shot it. It must have swum the river in its flight and the shooter didn't want to get wet in the cold water bad enough to follow it. The animals had been eating on it for several days as one side was completely laid open and was teeming with flies and maggots. The wind shifted a little and how it stunk! Ewwww! We rode back to fresh air and the herd at a gallop.

As we loped back to the herd, off to the west in the short grass, I saw something black moving along the ground. It wasn't that far away, but I couldn't tell what it was. Maybe a badger, except it was too dark to be a badger. It was about the size of a badger or a little bigger. We rode closer. It looked like a fuzzy ball whirling along the ground like a little whirlwind. I'd never seen anything like it, but I still couldn't tell what it was. We rode closer.

Skunks! It was a momma skunk and eight baby skunks. The momma was walking along looking for food perhaps, and the babies were all running around her in a tight circle. All the babies were running around momma at full speed and staying right up against her. It looked like a little whirlwind and the babies were so cute.

Uh-oh. Momma stops and is now looking at us. Time to go.

Ropin' and brandin'
Sunday, April 4, 1880

At breakfast, Porter said, "We'll be in Dodge City in a couple of weeks. This morning we'll brand any cattle we've picked up along the way. Any steer that doesn't have a herd brand on its left shoulder, we'll put one there. Willie, you and Bird will do the wrestlin'. Matthew the brandin'. Charley, you be the heeler. Hollis, get the brandin' iron out of your wagon and build up the fire. The rest of you, saddle your ponies and go bring 'em in.

I still hadn't done much roping so this was going to be fun – assuming I could actually find an unbranded steer, rope it and drag it to the fire without getting us gored. I saddled Nellie, uncoiled my rope and moved slowly out into the herd along with the other men. There's one! I shook out the rope into a noose, swung it over my head as we moved in closer and threw it over the steer's head. One side of the noose landed on top the steer's right horn and the other underneath its left horn. Nellie stopped, bringing the rope up tight – and the steer just walked out from under it all. I needed to make my loop bigger.

We kept after that steer. It took me three more throws before I was able to get the rope around its horns. It wasn't a very big calf. Not as old as the ones we were driving. I looped my end of the rope around the saddle horn and turned back toward the camp fire. Uh-oh, we turned the wrong way! The calf was on the other side of Nellie and the rope was cutting across my leg. Owwww! I walked toward the calf to loosen the rope so I could hold it up over Nellie's head. We turned the other way and I made a mental note to pay more attention which way to turn next time. We dragged the calf over to the campfire. It didn't want to go.

The boys were just finishing with a calf when we arrived. "Pull 'em on in close to the fire, Cory!" yelled Charley. Then Charley roped the hind legs of the calf. Bird and Willie were on top of it immediately. As Charley and I pulled the calf in different directions, it started to fall. Bird and Willie made sure it fell on its right side, but not too hard, and they held it tight as Matthew branded its left shoulder with the Rockin' P. "Maaaaa!" cried the calf and the smell of burning flesh filled the air.

Bird and Willie let loose the ropes turning the calf free and it fled back to the safety of the herd. I went back to hunting unbranded stock. There's one! It was a big steer. As big or maybe bigger than any of ours. Its horns were about six feet across. I made as big a noose as I could which didn't leave a lot of rope to throw so we rode in real close. He saw us coming and took off through the herd. We scattered cattle all over the place during our chase but we finally got close enough for me to throw my lasso. Perfect! Got 'em! I looped my end of the rope around the saddle horn and pulled Nellie to a stop. The rope drew tight and that big ol' steer kept running! Nellie had turned so the rope was on the right side with no danger of cutting across my leg. And that big chucklehead almost pulled us over.

He came to a stop with a jerk and swung around with his hind legs flying in the air. Then he took a bead on us and came at us. Uh-oh! Nellie saw the big steer coming at her and took off. There we were, the big roped steer chasing us through the herd. Cattle were scattering everywhere. I saw Albert just ahead and we headed for him. He saw what was happening and spurred his pony. As we flew by Albert, his noose went sailing through the air landing perfectly around the horns of the big steer. "Hold up, Cory!"

I pulled Nellie to a stop just as the big steer reached the end of Albert's rope. "Draw him up tight!" We turned and moved away so our rope was tight running the opposite direction. The steer was now trapped not being able to move in either direction. "let's take 'em in!" We kept the ropes tight and dragged that big ol' booger to the fire. Charley threw his rope so the steer stepped into his loop. Drawing it tight, the steer started to teeter. Willie and Bird grabbed it and it fell to the ground with a thud. 'sssssssssssssss"' sizzled the branding iron. "MAAAAAAAAAAA" went the big steer.

The boys unloosed our rope and I coiled mine up. "Boys, everybody better stand clear. This ol' boy's not gonna be too happy when he gets up," remarked Matthew. I rode a little ways off. That steer jumped to its feet and turned full circle twice looking for someone or something to charge. Not seeing an easy target, it trotted off back to the herd.

"That's the first time I seen a steer bring a cowboy to the brandin' iron," laughed Willie. Everyone laughed. Well, it probably was funny. I laughed too.

Albert rode by. "Not my first time, young cowboy," he said with a smile. "Boys, I believe that's it! I think we got them all." The other men had brought in and branded a dozen or so other steers while I brought in just those two. Oh well, I'm learning.

I found out later that during a normal roundup, the branding fire was close to the herd. The cowboys would rope just the hind legs of the calf and drag it to the fire where there were several cowboys assigned different duties. Two wrestlers to throw the calf if needed. One held its head. The other wrestler would put one of his feet on one of the calf's legs and pushed while pulling the other calf's leg back so the calf couldn't move. Then there was one man to brand the calf and one man to castrate the calf. Each man had his own assigned duty.

As I've mentioned before, we always referred to our herd of cattle as steers as we had no cows with us, but we had just as many heifers as steers.

Where's Porter?
Monday, April 5, 1880

That night as we finished up supper, Charley asked if anyone had seen Porter. No one had. It wasn't like him to get back to the herd after dark. He usually scouted ahead for a place to bed down for the night and, for planning our route for the next day so we wouldn't run into other nearby herds.

Cookie and Albert decided we should go looking for him. I wasn't on nighthawk duty that night so I volunteered to go. So it was me, Albert, Charley and Bird. Albert said to ride about a quarter mile apart and fire our pistol three times if we found anything. We were to ride northwesterly about two miles north of the River because that's where we thought Porter would have gone. It was real flat out there and during the day you could see for miles. With the half moon, we could occasionally see each other somewhat. I was on Paint and thought that if Porter was in trouble or possibly on foot he would need a ride back. So I caught Nellie, put a halter and lead rope on her and took her with me.

We rode slowly not knowing if he was on foot or down on the ground. The air was crisp and clear. I could hear an owl hooting from a dead cottonwood tree down on the river far away. Sound carries a long way on the prairie. We had gone about four miles when I heard three shots off to the north. I turned and rode that way to find Porter with Albert and Bird. Charley soon rode up behind me. Albert had spotted Porter walking and carrying his saddle. He had been carrying the saddle upside down on his back by the saddlehorn, along with his saddle blanket and rifle for several hours.

Come to find out, he had been scouting the way for the next day, when his pony was spooked by a covey of quail bursting up before them. Quail have a way of scaring the you know what out of you if you are not suspecting them. When a dozen or so of them all jump to flight right under your nose, it almost sounds like thunder. I've known guys to actually fall down while walking when this happens and even mess their britches.

Anyhow, Porter's pony spooked and took off on a mad dash to escape the perceived monster after him and ran right into a prairie dog town. As you might guess, he stepped into a prairie dog hole and broke his leg. Porter unsaddled him and then had to shoot him. There was no way to fix the pony's broken leg. He would suffer and eventually die. Porter then picked up his saddle and saddle blanket and slung them on his back. He picked up his rifle in the other hand and started walking back to the herd. He was pretty worn out when we found him.

We saddled up Nellie for him to ride and all of us except Bird headed back to camp. Bird rode off to the northwest. Who knows what he was up to? He still never talked.

For suppers, we usually had beans, bacon and sometimes biscuits or cornbread. If a steer got hurt and couldn't travel we'd have beef for a few days. But that had only happened once. Sometimes Cookie or someone else would bring in a turkey, rabbit or squirrel they had shot during the day and he would cook the meat in with the beans. That next night and for the next couple of days, there were some pretty big chunks of meat in with the beans. The meat actually tasted a little sweeter than beef.

It took me several days to realize just what it was.

Stampede!
Tuesday, April 6, 1880

Under Porter's direction, we kept the herd well south of the prairie dog town. I could see what was left of Porter's pony. You could tell the coyotes and other critters had been feasting on it. Well one man's loss is a bunch of critters' gain! I could hear the prairie dogs chirping their warnings to the other prairie dogs as we passed by. There were hundreds of them. The prairie dog town probably covered about five acres or more. Soon after we passed, I could hear some popping back that way. It sounded like shots from a light gun. Later on in the afternoon, Porter rode by and he was carrying my .32 rifle. "Nice gun, Cory." I could tell he was still mad about losing his pony.

Today was another day that just felt ominous. It was warmer than it had been in several days and the wind was blowing strong out of the southwest. There were lots of fluffy white clouds in the sky. Toward evening there were some lower clouds that seemed to be going in the opposite direction. We were still keeping the herd on a northwest course and were staying a couple miles north of the river. I was at my usual post along the left flank having to push the steers a little as the grass was new and green. The tenderest kind. All these cattle wanted to do was stop and eat.

Driving cattle is not a quiet job. Those critters moo and bawl all of the time. All day and most of the night. A body gets used to it after a while, I suppose. On this day I could hear cattle back behind us. It was still real flat, so soon I could see another herd not too far behind us, and between us and the river. I hadn't seen them before so they must be pushing their cattle harder and faster than we were. Most likely not stopping on Sundays either to rest like we were.

145

Their trail boss must be determined to be one of the first herds to Dodge City.

Getting close to sundown, we turned the herd south toward the river so they could get their evening drink. The other herd had just passed us by, so we were able to come in behind them. We sure didn't want to get the herds mixed together. What a mess that would be. The north slope of the river was fairly gentle and the herd was able to spread out somewhat to get to the water so it didn't take very long for them all to drink.

After all of the steers and the ponies had had their fill, we turned them back to the north and then pushed northwest just a little farther to some fresh untrampled grass. Here we turned the leaders back into the herd and bunched them all up. By now they all knew the routine and I'm sure they were ready to stop for the day.

The sky was getting dark and it was due to some huge tall clouds building up to our south and west. The clouds blocked out the sun so it seemed darker earlier than usual. Our cattle settled down and didn't seem to pay the clouds much mind. I could see lightning in the tops of some of the clouds. The cloud closest to us had a long anvil on the top stretching out for miles it seemed and the cloud seemed to grow taller and taller each time I looked that way.

The herd to our south had bedded down due south of ours and more than a mile away. They were pretty close to the river, probably just out of the sand hills. Glancing that way occasionally, I didn't notice many of them settling down. They were probably hungry as it didn't appear they got to eat much as they traveled and there wasn't as much grass that close to the river. Porter came riding up to the chuckwagon, "Fellows, I went over to visit the herd south of us. McKnight is their trail boss. I know him. He always thinks he has to get to Dodge City first to get the best prices. They've been pushing their cattle too hard. They all look rather gaunt and maybe are a little more irritable than usual." Longhorns aren't known for their pleasant dispositions, mainly because few have one. "We may have storms tonight, so we will double the nighthawks and try to keep the herd calm. Every man will take a four hour shift."

Albert started assigning everyone a time to ride. Since there was only 10 of us and there were to be four on each shift, we weren't going to get but a few hours' sleep tonight if we're lucky to get that much. Oh well, the life of a cowboy. I was assigned the second shift with Bird, Willie and Charley.

When you know you have to be up in a few hours, it's impossible to get to sleep no matter how tired you are. I know some of the guys can be asleep in minutes after laying down. There was something in the air tonight that made me uneasy. I just couldn't fall asleep.

All of a sudden, Charley was shaking me, "Cory, time to go. Let's ride!" I was instantly awake. It felt like I hadn't fallen asleep at all. I actually felt more tired than when I first laid down. I saddled Star, tied my slicker behind my saddle in case in stormed, and rode out to start circling the herd. I rode clockwise that night. Willie was riding clockwise too, so he was always on the opposite side of the herd. I would pass Bird or Charley about every 15 minutes or so. Because of the clouds, I couldn't see the stars and know what time it was. Charley had gone by four times, so I figured we had been out about an hour, so it was around one a.m. There was some thunder and quite a bit of lightning. It didn't seem to be of much concern to our steers.

Coming around the herd to the south, I saw it all happen.

147

There must have been a real tall cottonwood tree down by the river real close to where McKnight's herd was. I saw the bolt of lightning hit tree and then there was a huge boom right overhead ten seconds later. Our steers jumped to their feet. A minute later I heard more thunder. Rolling thunder. Then I realized, that thunder wasn't stopping. It was actually getting louder. Oh no, stampede! It was McKnight's herd and it was heading right for us. I raced back to camp, "Stampede from the south! Stampede from the south!" Men jumped out of their bedrolls and ran for their mounts without bothering to get dressed. Our herd had also heard them coming and had started running to the north and then McKnight's herd hit us. A wave of 2,000 steers running full out slammed into our 2,400 head. Star and I were caught up in the flood of horns and cowhide.

Before I knew it, I was in the middle of a mass of horns and cattle running hell bent for leather. Lord only knows where to. If Star got gored or stepped into a hole, I was a goner. I held on to the saddle horn with my right hand so I wouldn't fall off if he shied unexpectantly. I tried to guide Star toward the edge of the herd, the edge of which now seemed very far away in any direction. I was galloping full speed in the middle of a mass of 4 - 5,000 crazed longhorns! I could see a rider not too far in front of me and to my left, also riding for his life. I started working my way that direction.

About that time, we must of run into the herd that had been off to our north. It was so dark that I couldn't make out anything but the cattle within a few feet of me, unless there was a lightning flash. There were gaps in the mad dash now instead of solid steers since some of McKnight's cattle were tiring. I was getting closer to the rider to tell that it was Willie.

All of a sudden, a big steer took exception to Willie's pony being so close and rammed its three foot long horn right into Willie's pony's belly. There was a loud scream and the steer, pony and Willie all went down in the middle of all of those churning hooves. Willie had leaped off his pony to keep from getting pinned under it. Two steps and I was right on top of him. Switching the reins to my right hand, I grabbed Willie under his right arm near his armpit with my left arm, he clamped his hand onto my arm and I leaned backwards as far as I could pulling him up behind me. He grabbed me around the waist and we both held onto Star for dear life.

I was unable to move through the mass of steers any more to the left so we continued north with the herd matching it stride for stride. I was afraid we would go down any minute. After several miles the cattle began to tire and slow down. The panic was over and we were finally able to get away from the flow of the stampede. We pulled up out of the mass of steers and sat there as the last of the steers finally trotted by. Star's head was hanging low and Willie and I were both shaking uncontrollably.

I remember in church, the preacher talked about Hell being fire and brimstone (whatever brimstone is). I always had the idea that Hell was hot and that if you were bad and went to Hell, you burned for eternity. I could imagine what that might be like as I have been badly sunburned and have burned my hand on the stove. After that night, my idea of Hell was being caught in night time stampede of crazed longhorns for an eternity with the constant threat of being thrown, trampled, and gored. I still have nightmares about that night.

"C-c-c-Cory? You s-s-s-saved my life," Wille stuttered. "I'll n-n-n-never be able to r-r-r-repay you."

All I could think of was, "How 'bout you quit pickin' on Hollis?"

Willie stuck out his hand. We shook.

Willie not only never picked on Hollis again, the three of us became great friends.

Star had given his all to save all three of us and seemed on the verge of collapsing. His legs were wide apart and his chest was heaving. Plus, he had many bloody gashes from the horns that had grazed him during the frightful run. My pants were ripped to shreds below the knees and my legs between my knees and my boots were bloody as well. Willie and I climbed off Star and the three of us started the long slow walk back to camp. Hoping it was still there and not crushed under 10,000 hooves. It took us two hours before we stumbled into camp. All three of us were plumb tuckered out.

The camp, chuckwagon and supply wagon were all safe and untouched. (With the next morning's light we found the dirt churned up within 50 feet of the chuckwagon). As I unsaddled Star, Willie was telling everyone how I had ridden across the stampede to snatch him from the hooves of death. I had never been so wore out in my whole life.

"Cory, I'll take care of your pony for you."

"Thanks, Hollis." I dropped my saddle on the ground where we stood and laid down right there on the bare ground, my head on the saddle for a pillow.

The last thing I remember was Porter saying something like, "I told you he'd never quit."

Separating the herds
April 7, 8, 9

I felt like I had hardly fallen asleep when daylight woke me. The other men, except for Willie, had their ponies saddled and ready to go. Porter was talking, "Boys, I have good news and bad news. The good news is there are 40 cowboys ready to roundup and cut out three herds of cattle." Everyone groaned. "The bad news is there are about 7,000 of them. Let's get to work and get them sorted.

We'll push ours over here toward the wagons. McKnight is going to push his further along the trail and back toward the river to the northwest and Hodges men will push theirs to the north of us. Do the sorting by the trail brands. Each herd will have two men stationed south, west and north of the big bunch, once we get them all rounded up. Everyone else will do the sorting and push the cattle to them. The outriders will push them on toward their gathering point. Any questions?

Let's get to work.

Cory, once we start the sort, you and Willie stay on the south side of the big bunch. Whenever anyone brings you some steers, head them this way."

"Yes, sir!"

"Let's round 'em!"

I saddled Socks, and Willie and I rode out together. Good thing there was an extra saddle for Willie. Without a word spoken to each other, we both rode directly to the spot where Willie's pony had fallen. There wasn't much left of his saddle or his pony. Both had been trampled to bits. "I could have ended up looking like that saddle if it wasn't for you, Cory."

"We were both very lucky."

Looking out over the stampede area, there were more than a couple dozen dead animals. Albert came riding up and surveyed what we had been looking at. "Willie, is that what's left of your saddle and your pony?"

"Yup."

"You're one lucky guy."

"Yup."

"Porter said that Hodges had paid toll tax to a Cherokee Indian yesterday afternoon. No one has seen him today. You might keep an eye out. He might look just like that saddle today."

It took us three days to round up and sort the cattle. It was easy to sort McKnight's steers, they were noticeably thinner than ours or Hodges. It got to where we didn't even have to look at the herd brand. Charley's final tally ended up with us six head short. Not bad considering all the dead carcasses and those that were lost. We did find two live steers with broken legs so all camps will have fresh beef tonight.

We are to push ahead tomorrow, Saturday. Thank goodness the day after is Sunday.

I don't know if the steers need a day's rest, but all of the men and the ponies sure do.

Bat smoke
Saturday, April 10, 1880

We took it slow today. Very slow. We were still trying to catch our breath from the past three days, plus Porter wanted to let that crazy McKnight get way ahead of us. He said that if McKnight's cattle would have been in better shape, they may not have spooked so easily. I'm glad that we had branded those mavericks a few days ago. We would have had a hard time claiming them between the three herds. There were a few head that didn't have a herd brand on them and Porter and Hodges decided to let McKnight have them since a good portion of the dead steers were from his herd.

Since we were traveling two miles from the river and parallel, we had to drive the herd two miles to the river every day. Once in the evening and again in the morning for them to drink. This took several hours each time. The good thing was the river sloped gently from the north and it was easy to get to, so the cattle could line up alongside each other instead of having to wait their turn like they did when crossing a creek on narrow trails. Occasionally, we would find a steer or heifer that had been left behind by another herd.

That morning when we took the cattle to the river, we could see to the southeast across the river what looked to be large sand dunes. There didn't appear to be any vegetation of any kind on them. Just hills and hills of sand. Tall hills. It looked just like the Great Sahara Desert I had read about in school, just a lot smaller.

As we were waiting on the herd to get their evening drinks from the Cimarron that evening, Charley said, "Look over there. Smoke!" We all looked to the west to see a slight column of smoke rising from the nearby hills.

"That's not smoke. Those are bats!" Albert exclaimed.

"Yeah boy!"

Sure enough. A few flew overhead and close enough by that we could see them. Little bitty things. Fluttering in the sky. Soon they had all disappeared and I couldn't tell where they had gone.

Maybe we could go find the bat cave tomorrow!

As the sun set, I could make out what looked to be an owl flying low toward the river.

Now that I think about it, there was a red sky this morning and I don't remember the wind blowing much at all today. Don't guess that saying works every time.

The cave
Sunday, April 11, 1880

After taking the herd to the river for water this morning, and the two miles back to where there was good grass for them to graze today, Hollis, Willie, Bird and I took our turns watching the herd during the morning shifts. After lunch, we all rode west in search of the bat cave. We crossed over to the other side of the shallow Cimarron to find a completely different terrain. The north and east side of the river was rolling sand hills along the river and then very flat away from it. The south and west side of the river was very rough and very hilly. We rode straight west to where we thought the bats came from, looking for something that might be their cave.

Around noon and about five miles from the river, we were on top of some hills and came upon what looked like a small canyon. Hollis and I rode along one side with Bird and Willie on the other. The sides of the canyon were cliffs and very steep with a few places here and there that a person might be able to climb down. We were looking for some kind of break in the solid rock. Something that might indicate a cave. Thankfully, the few trees there had yet to leaf out.

After a couple hours of searching, Bird found what looked like the entrance to a cave down in the canyon right below us. It was about 30 feet below the top of the canyon wall, and the opening was about 12 feet high and 20 feet wide. We hobbled our ponies and climbed down into the canyon. Looking into the mouth of the cave, we could tell we were not the first people to find it. There was the remains of an old campfire and some trash. "White men," Bird said.

As we stepped into the shadow of the cave, we could see that it opened up very wide and appeared to go on. We could tell that it was deeper than you could see from the outside and we could feel a cool breeze blowing in our faces. No one had thought to bring any matches or candles or anything we could light our way with. And none of us wanted to go very far into the dark. We all went in a little way and waited a few minutes for our eyes to adjust to the darkness. Then we went in a little further. We were able to walk in about 100 feet or more before it got too dark to see as the opening was fairly large. We didn't see any evidence of bats though we found evidence of the cave being used by others.

"Outlaws," said Willie. "What other white men would ever be in this area where they had to spend the night in a cave?"

"Good point." I hope our ponies are alright and none of those outlaws are around now.

We hiked out of the cave. Hollis and I climbed back up our side of the canyon, and we all continued our hunt for the bat cave. As the sun started to head down in the western sky, we turned back toward our camp so we could help the rest of the men take the herd to water that evening.

We never did find the bat cave, unless that was it and the bats came out a different entrance. Although we kept an eye to the western sky that evening, we didn't see the bats again. They must have gone a different way that night.

The Battle of Turkey Creek
Monday, April 12, 1880

After watering the herd, we had them on the move by mid-morning. They were back to moving in good fashion being led by Homer. He had survived the stampede without any serious injuries, cuts or scrapes. Some of the other steers had wide gashes along their sides, and there were more stragglers than usual.

The terrain was getting a little more hilly as we went and the steers were back to traveling about 2-3 wide instead of more spread out like during the past week. The line of 2,400 steers stretched out for a half mile or better. We let them walk and casually graze.

At the mid-day break, we crossed Turkey Creek. Albert said there had been a big Indian battle a few miles north of us at Turkey Springs just a year and a half ago on September 13 & 14, 1878. He hadn't heard of any Indian battles around these parts since then. Albert said that Cheyennes under Little Wolf and Dull Knife had fled the reservation at the Darlington Agency, where we had earlier passed nearby, and were trying to get back to their homes in the Dakotas when they came across these two cowboys who they promptly killed. The cowboys worked on a ranch in Kansas and were heading down to the salt flats on the Cimarron with a wagon and team of mules.

The Fourth Cavalry out of Fort Reno had been pursuing the renegades and caught up to the Cheyennes at Turkey Springs. A fierce battle in the nearby canyons and hills resulted in three cavalrymen and five Indians killed. The chase continued through Kansas and into Nebraska where the Indians were finally captured and taken to Fort Robinson. Albert said this bunch of Indians were

Northern Cheyenne and were trying to get back to their families.

Later, the two cowboys' bodies were found nearby full of arrows. Albert said he had found the grave markers of two cowboys on last year's drive.

Just a year and a half ago! Ugh! A chill went down my spine. There's nothing to say some more Indians down on the nearby reservation might want to make another break for it and kill anyone they came across. As a matter of fact, these same Indians are probably down there now just waiting for the chance to sneak off again.

I'm going to try to sleep with one eye open again tonight.

Leaving the Cimarron
Tuesday, April 13, 1880

After following the Cimarron northwest for so many days, it made a sharp turn to the west where a good size creek came in from the north. Albert said this was Bluff Creek and that we were now in Kansas. We will continue north northwest along Bluff Creek toward Dodge City. We were about two days out.

The land was so flat here that a body could stand on a gopher hill and see into the next county. This had been Pawnee country up until seven years ago. They had been moved onto a reservation down in Indian Territory back in '73.

The cattle were moving along at a nice walk stopping here and there to grab a mouthful of grass. None seemed interested in turning back to Indian Territory. And none had a clue as to what fate awaited them in Dodge City. I was riding Paint with my knee wrapped around the saddlehorn and slumping in the saddle.

There were two red-tailed hawks circling in the air high above us. As I was watching the hawks, one of the hawks began to spiral downward in a lazy fashion. Down and down and down until it landed not 30 yards from us. I pulled Paint to a stop to watch what had got the hawk's attention. Usually a hawk will swoop down upon some unsuspecting rodent and catch it in its talons. It will sit there for a few moments until its meal is secure and then it flies away to some treetop or nest to eat. Not this hawk.

It stood there on the ground staring intently at something on the ground which I could not see. Paint and I sat still and patiently waited and watched. I think Paint also sensed something unusual was happening or fixin' to happen as he had his ears pointed in that direction.

After a few hops here and there, the hawk, and it was a big red-tailed hawk, spread its wings. They had to be five feet across. With us still watching, the hawk bent its wings forward a little bit and then flapped one wing and then the other just a little bit – and then it sprang up slightly in the air and straight down again.

With the hawk engrossed in its battle with whatever it was, Paint and I moved in a little closer. It was a snake! I could see the head of the snake in the hawk's mouth and it was much bigger than its neck. It had to be a rattlesnake! The big red-tailed hawk had killed a rattlesnake! I had never heard of such a thing. I wouldn't have believed anyone who had told me a hawk would kill a rattlesnake except I saw it with my own two eyes.

Paint and I were within 15 yards of the hawk and the snake, just sitting there when the hawk finally noticed us. It sprang into the air with the snake in its talons. I'm guessing that rattlesnake was a good three or four feet long.

Good riddance to the snake!

Harley
Wednesday, April 14, 1880

Harley had never fully recovered from his illness of a couple of weeks ago. He had been coughing continuously and always seemed to be bent over spitting up something. This morning as we were finishing breakfast and fixin' to take the cattle over to the creek for watering, I noticed Harley hadn't gotten up yet. It wasn't unusual for him to be the first one in bed and the last one up, but I sensed something was not quite right. As I was saddling Nellie, I saw Hollis walk over to where he slept, "Harley. Time to rise and shine!"

"Harley?" No answer. No movement. I led Nellie over to Hollis. Harley was laying on his side facing away from the fire of last night. I reached down to shake him and he rolled over toward me. His eyes were open in a stare that I immediately realized wasn't a stare. I had never seen a dead person this close before. It was unsettling. Especially if you're not expecting it.

"Albert! Mr. Porter!"

"Yeah, Cory. What's the matter? Can't get ol' Harley up this morning?"

"I think ol' Harley's gotten up for the last time."

Sure enough, ol' Harley was dead. "He was just plain wore out," said Albert. "Lord knows how old he was. Probably not as old as he looks. He'd been takin' cattle to Missouri and Kansas since before the War, and some years on up into Nebraska and Wyoming. He once told me he'd rather trail cattle than dig fence posts in hard ground."

161

Harley had told us stories around the campfire at night about cattle drives up the Shawnee Trail to Kansas and Missouri. Crossing the Red at Colbert's Ferry. Up past Fort Washita, Boggy Depot and Fort Gibson. Up and around all the big hills. Driving cattle that didn't want to go, through trees and Indian settlements. Fighting outlaws, thieves and settlers to get to the railheads.

One of my favorite stories of Harley's was a drive to Abilene back in '68 or '69. They crossed the Red about 30 miles downstream from Red River Station. The River was up and over a half mile across. It took two days to build a raft to ferry their wagon across. During the crossing, they lost over a hundred head and one man drowned. The cattle were driven to the west of the Arbuckle Mountains and around the north side to Fort Arbuckle on Wildhorse Creek near the Washita River. Albert told us that the Arbuckles were once as tall as the snow-capped Rockies out west, but nobody believed him. The herd crossed the Canadian near the old site of Choteau's Trading Post, where Jesse Chisholm had a trading post. It was downstream a ways from where we crossed it at Silver City. The Trail then joined what is now the Chisholm Trail south of the Cimarron.

We buried Harley right there. Funny thing about Albert's remark about the fence posts and hard ground, the ground we buried him in was as hard as ground can be without it being solid rock I think. We all took turns with the one shovel Cookie had in the supply wagon and it took us two hours or better to dig his grave about three foot deep. We hit rock then and had no way of going deeper, so we wrapped him in his blanket and lowered him in the hole.

"Lord, take this old drover and make him comfortable. He was a good man and a dependable hand. He spent the last years of his life driving cattle so the folks east of the Mississippi could eat," prayed Porter.

"Amen," we all said together.

Willie and I shoveled dirt back into the hole and covered him up good. There were no trees in sight, so there was no way to make a cross or mark the grave. A few years from now, no one will ever know that ol' Harley lays here.

With Harley gone and us close to Dodge City, we moved the cattle more in a bunch than all strung out so that Bird and I riding flank could also move behind them occasionally and keep them moving. Good thing it was pretty flat with just slight rolling hills. The cattle didn't have to wind their way around taller hills single file or even two or three wide.

I remember it warming up pretty good that day with scattered clouds in the sky. The night was going to cool down fast once the sun went down.

Sleepy Hollis
Thursday, April 15, 1880

This morning seemed like a repeat of yesterday morning, except this morning it was Hollis who wouldn't get up. I had saddled Socks and was getting ready to ride out to help take the cattle over to the creek for water. "Hollis! Hollis! Rise and shine. Or are you dead too?" No response. That's odd. Hollis usually got up when Cookie did and helped him prepare breakfast.

"I went over and kicked him a while ago to come help me," Cookie said, "and he never moved a muscle. I guess he's just gettin' lazy like everyone else."

"Hollis? Hollis? Time to get goin' partner." No response. I got this feeling of dread. It was yesterday all over again. What's that called – déjà vu?

I bent over and pulled the cover off his face. He was laying on his back. His eyes were wide open. I thought, oh no. Not again! Then his eyes moved and looked right at me. I noticed his forehead was beaded with sweat. "Hollis, what's wrong?"

Without turning his head or moving a muscle, he mouthed 'snake'. "Hollis, do you have a snake in there with you?" He mouthed 'yes. Really? Criminy! "I'll be right back." Everyone had already ridden off but Cookie was still there pulling down the canvas porch he had put up the evening before in front of the chuckwagon.

"Cookie! Cookie! Hollis has a snake there in bed with him. What do we do? If it's a rattler, it might bite him and then he'll die too."

"The days are warmin' up and the snakes must be movin' about. One must have gotten chilly last night and decided to snuggle up to poor Hollis to stay warm. Tell you what we'll do. I'll get the shovel and you pull the covers off Hollis real nice and slow. If it's a rattlesnake, I'll try to get the shovel between his head and Hollis, then you can roll Hollis off the other way. Savvy?"

"Yep." I was so nervous, I was shaking. I didn't want to be the cause of Hollis getting snakebit. "Hollis, you lie perfectly still. I'm goin' to pull the covers back real slow so we can get a good look at your friend there. When we're ready, I'm goin' to help you roll out of the way. Got it?"

Hollis mouthed another 'yes'. His face was as white as a cloud. "Which side is he on? This side? 'Yes', he mouthed without moving a muscle. "He's on this side, Cookie."

"Good thing he wasn't on my side when I kicked Hollis earlier to wake him up!"

I stood on Hollis' right side and slowly pulled the cover up, hoping I didn't get bit as well. I first saw the rattle right below Hollis' shoulder. Nine rattles. It was a big one.

"It's a rattler, Cookie!"

"Alright, Cory, nice and slow. It looks like it is stretched out alongside him. That's good. If he was coiled up, he could strike half the length of his body." The rattle started buzzing. "Wait a minute! Hold up!" I froze with the covers down to Hollis' chest. "He's movin'! Maybe he'll crawl out on his own." Cookie moved up toward Hollis' head. We waited. The snake was kind of a brownish grayish color with a gold stripe running the length of his body. There were also black bands a couple inches apart. Except for the fact that it was a poisonous snake that could possibly kill Hollis, it was kinda pretty in a wild animal way.

No one moved for about ten minutes and then we saw the snake poke his head out from under the covers near Hollis' feet. Still no one moved. The snake crawled out another foot where he was past Hollis' feet and suddenly Cookie plunged the shovel into the ground right behind the snake's head lopping it off. I grabbed Hollis and pulled him toward me and we both fell in a heap. Getting up slowly, I could see that Hollis was still shaking. He sank back to his knees. "You better get goin', Cory. They'll be wonderin' where ya are."

"Watch the head, it can still bite you," Cookie warned. He stabbed at the rattlesnake's head with the shovel until it had been pounded into the ground. He then put a rock over it.

"Okey doke." That was a tough row to hoe. I didn't realize that I too was shaking somewhat until I pulled myself up into the saddle. I rode out to see that the cattle were being herded back away from Bluff Creek and were getting started on their way to the cowpens at Dodge City. Their last day on the trail.

"Where ya been, Cory?" asked Albert as I rode up. I told him about Hollis and the rattlesnake. "Sounds like a timber rattler. Funny how you'll find them out here on the prairie. Must've gotten caught out in the cold last night. Glad Hollis is alright. Let's get these steers to Dodge!"

We halted the herd on the Arkansas River about three miles southeast of town and not too far from Fort Dodge. We had a couple hours of daylight left, but Porter said the loading pens were full. He had already been into Dodge City and had contracted the cattle for sale at $39 a head.

166

So all we had to do in the morning was drive them into the loading pens, count them, and we were through.

We went ahead and took the cattle down to the river for their evening drink. There wasn't much water in the Arkansas. Then we drove them straight west and closer to town for the night. This will be my last night to nighthawk. I have the midnight to two am shift.

I was the last one in from bedding down the steers. I got there just in time to hear Hollis telling everyone about the six foot long rattlesnake in his bed that was as big as his leg. Cookie was standing to the side shaking his head and holding his arms about three feet apart. Anyway, I was glad it wasn't me. I was going to make sure there are no holes in my bedroll that any critter could move in without me knowing it!

Cookie made biscuits this evening and brought out a jar of sorghum. "Savin' it for a special occasion," he said. It sure was good. I think I got the last couple of spoonfuls.

Last day
Friday, April 16, 1880

Today feels like a holiday. All of the hands were of unusual good humor and we took the steers to the Arkansas for one last drink. There wasn't much water in the river again this morning, but the cattle were able to spread out for quite a ways so it didn't take too long to get them watered. We had them all in the loading pens by the railroad and cattle cars by mid-morning.

"I counted 9,620 legs today, Cory. Yeah boy!", Charley said with a grin. "At $39 a head, Porter will have a whole bunch of money in his pocket in no time! And so will we!"

Porter came into camp around noon that day. The final tally had agreed with Charley's count, of course, and Porter had been given some cash and a bank draft for the herd from the buyer. These steers will be in Chicago or a packing plant somewhere east in just a few days. I hated to see the last of Homer. We didn't get off to a good start, but he was the best lead steer all through Indian Territory.

We had been on the trail for 45 days, not counting today, since I joined the herd in Spanish Fort. "Cory, here is $45. That's a dollar a day plus a $5 bonus less the $5 advance I gave you when you went to Duncan's Store. Also, you can keep the saddle you've been using. You'll need a pony to go under it, I suppose?"

"Yes sir."

Porter continued, "We picked up six extra steers along the way. For your share you can take one of the ponies you've been riding. It's yours if you'd like. You've earned it."

"Thank you, sir. I'll take the palomino mare."

Porter turned to walk away. Then stopped and turned back, "Oh, one more thing, Cory. You can have the rifle and one of the pistols we took from the horse thieves, if you want them. You saved our ponies and kept any of us from getting shot. It's only right that you should have them.

I was stunned. I had a rig now for my very own – a good mare, a saddle, bedroll, rifle, another pistol - and $45 in my pocket. Wow! I felt rich!

Later on, Albert came in and sat down at the table where Willie, Bird, Hollis and I were eating lunch at the Wright House. I was on my third cup of Whitman's Instantaneous Chocolate. I'd never had anything like this before! Man that was good stuff! I couldn't get enough of it.

"Boys, there's a man in town that is lookin' for men to take a herd of cows, heifers and bulls to Wyoming. Whaddaya say?"

My first thought was how many weeks I had been on the trail. I missed Papa and Mama. Johnnie and little Ida. Almost all of these past weeks, it had been either cold or windy, or both. Cold or wet, or both. Dusty and windy for the most part. Then all the hours in the saddle. All the late nights on nighthawk. The nights with not enough sleep. The stampede. The boring food. Yes, generally miserable most of the time. And dead tired all of the time.

My second thought was how hot Texas can be in the summer.

"Sure. Why not?"

Postscript

Cornelius worked on a couple of cattle ranches and saved his money. In 1887, he bought some cattle and moved across the Red River into Indian Territory on Mud Creek near present day Grady, Oklahoma, where he spent the first night with the herd. He leased land, farmed and raised cattle. He and Lizzie were married in 1891. Seven of their thirteen children were born in Indian Territory. In 1901, they moved near Spanish Fort, Texas where Cornelius bought 761 acres in the area where he first met with the cattle herd. By 1906, they owned 1,004 acres. In 1932 Cornelius helped move his second oldest son, Robert Valentine, by wagon to a homestead near the high hill by the nameless creek where he sat on his horse and saw the "best grass in the country." (Five miles southeast of present day Waurika, Oklahoma in Jefferson County). Valentine lived there 56 years and a grandson lives there still. His oldest son, Albert, lived three miles east and south of Valentine. Cornelius died in 1935 from complications after being kicked by a horse.

■■■

By Kevin D. Howard

■■■

Special thanks to Patty, my navigator, editor and best friend.

Family notes

The names, ages and postscript of Cornelius and his family are fact.

March 4, 1880 – all locations mentioned are on the Chisholm Trail. The nameless creek is just south of Granddad's ranch house. The tall hill and the wagon tracks are in the South Pasture.

March 9, 1880 – Lookout Hill, now referred to as Monument Hill, is east of Addington, Oklahoma. There is now a tall granite monument overlooking and commemorating the Chisholm Trail.

March 11, 1880 – Duncan's Station was located near the intersection of present day north/south Highway 81 and east/west Highway 7. Highway 7 is the route of the old military road between Fort Arbuckle and Ft. Sill. Highway 81 generally follows the old Chisholm Trail.

There were five Marlow brothers who lived around the Marlow, Oklahoma area. A cave where they hid out, has been found where the town is now. Three of them, including Llewelyn, were killed in a gunfight in 1889.

March 12, 1880 – the names of the rivers and creeks in the story are real. Rush Creek's headwaters are from Rush Springs, near the town of Rush Springs, Oklahoma.

March 15, 1880 – the Fred Trading Post was run by Col. Frank Fred and was located a few miles south of Chickasha, Oklahoma. The rock bottom crossing of the Washita River was a few miles east of Chickasha.

March 16, 1880 – Silver City was a trading post about eight miles east of present day Minco, Oklahoma and 2-3 miles north of Tuttle, Oklahoma on the south side of the Canadian River.

Pikey's Crossing is now the site of the Highway 4 bridge crossing the Canadian River.

March 17 - 19, 1880 – the east branch of the Chisholm Trail crossed the Canadian River near the present town of Mustang, Oklahoma (our first home) and continued north through the present location of Yukon, Oklahoma. The midday break in the story was at the site of our home north of Piedmont, near Taylor's Hill where we watched many Easter sunrises. From here, the Chisholm Trail angled back to the northwest to meet back up with the west branch of the Trail near present day Dover, Oklahoma on the Cimarron River.

March 27, 1880 – Bullfoot Station is now the townsite of Hennessey, Oklahoma. The stage station at Skeleton Ranch is now the town of Enid, Oklahoma. The spring referred at Skeleton is the headwaters of Skeleton Creek which joins the Cimarron just south of Mulhall, Oklahoma.

April 10, 1880 – the sand dunes were where Little Sahara State Park is now. The bats were from the nearby Selman bat cave near Freedom, Oklahoma, where currently resides 500,000 Mexican free-tail bats.

April 11, 1880 – the cave the boys discovered is Alabaster Caverns.

April 16, 1880 –also one of my favorite holidays. One of my favorite horses was Granddad's palomino, Nellie.

Cornelius named his sons Albert, Robert, William, Hollis, Charley, and Matthew.

Spanish Fort – Cornelius and Lizzy are buried in the Liberty Chapel cemetery southeast of Spanish Fort.

About the Author

Kevin is a CPA in Oklahoma and Texas. He and his wife, Patty, took their children on vacation to all 50 states. They have visited 55 of America's 58 national parks that are located in the States. A few of Kevin's hobbies include hiking in the deserts and in the mountains, shooting replicas of Old West pistols and rifles, working and hiking on their land, and of course, visiting, hiking and playing with his kids and grandkids. He has hiked to the bottom of the Grand Canyon a dozen times, including Rim-to-Rim-to-Rim, and has summited 48 of Colorado's 54 highest peaks.